HAVE YOU EVER WONDERED WHAT HAPPENED TO that little ugly duckling after he became a beautiful swan? I have. (Yes, I know there are more important things in life to ponder, like the new world order, reducing the deficit, and whether we *really* can get a perfect cup of coffee each time, every time. But let's face it, that swan had to have had some rebound problems.)

Did he really live happily ever after? Did the other swans now laugh because he once thought he was a duck? Did he feel the need to swim past Ducktown every so often, just to prove he wasn't a geek to the bully duckies? Or is it "ducky bullies"? But most of all, did he still feel like that ugly duckling inside, no matter how good the outside now looked?

We all know the package has nothing to do with the gift inside, where it really counts toward a person of worth. But no matter what our inside/outside packaging, all of us have felt like ugly ducklings upon occasion, and for some, no matter how much one grows as a person, those feelings are never quite resolved. Unless there's love. With a little love, self-esteem can get that final push over the hill to the "I'm Okay, You're Okay" valley of contentment. And maybe we still haven't seen in ourselves what someone who loves us has seen all along: a beautiful swan.

So that's why I've always wondered about that swan. Was he getting enough vitamins and did he know how beautiful he was on the inside from the moment he hatched from the egg? I hope you enjoy *He's So Shy*.

WHAT ARE *LOVESWEPT* ROMANCES?

They are stories of true romance and touching emotion. We believe those two very important ingredients are constants in our highly sensual and very believable stories in the LOVESWEPT line. Our goal is to give you, the reader, stories of consistently high quality that may sometimes make you laugh, sometimes make you cry, but are always fresh and creative and contain many delightful surprises within their pages.

Most romance fans read an enormous number of books. Those they truly love, they keep. Others may be traded with friends and soon forgotten. We hope that each LOVESWEPT romance will be a treasure—a "keeper." We will always try to publish

LOVE STORIES YOU'LL NEVER FORGET
BY AUTHORS YOU'LL ALWAYS REMEMBER

The Editors

Loveswept 664

HE'S SO SHY

LINDA CAJIO

BANTAM BOOKS

NEW YORK · TORONTO · LONDON · SYDNEY · AUCKLAND

HE'S SO SHY
A Bantam Book / January 1994

If you would be interested in receiving protective vinyl covers for your
Loveswept books, please write to this address for information:

Loveswept
Bantam Books
P.O. Box 985
Hicksville, NY 11802

ISBN 0-553-44274-0

Published simultaneously in the United States and Canada

Bantam Books are published by Bantam Books, a division of Bantam Doubleday Dell Publishing Group, Inc. Its trademark, consisting of the words "Bantam Books" and the portrayal of a rooster, is Registered in U.S. Patent and Trademark Office and in other countries. Marca Registrada. Bantam Books, 1540 Broadway, New York, New York 10036.

PRINTED IN THE UNITED STATES OF AMERICA

OPM   0 9 8 7 6 5 4 3 2 1

Many thanks to JFC and DDL for the inspiration

PROLOGUE

1964

"Hey, Cretin!"

Richard Creighton froze. The voice could have belonged to any one of a hundred kids in the Penns Grove, New Jersey, Elementary School or, for that matter, it could have belonged to any of the kids in any of the five other schools he'd attended since kindergarten. It was the same everywhere. Everyone hated him. A few more steps up into the school building and he would have been safe, with teachers to protect him. He wished he could fly across space and into that safety zone. He wished his name were anything but Creighton. Somehow, even though he never said a word, the kids always tagged him Cretin—or worse. Why couldn't he have been named James

Garner or Bret Maverick? Now those were names to be proud of.

"It's the Cretin!" Billy Prescott said, coming into view. A bunch of boys gathered around behind him. Billy's toadies. "And he's wearing white socks today! White socks! White socks!"

Richard groaned. Billy was the worst bully he'd encountered yet. He wanted to run, but knew that if he did they'd beat him up. If he stood still and didn't lip off, he might get away with only giving up his lunch money. Kids passed him and went into school, some giggling at his latest humiliation, some pretending not to see what was happening. No one helped. It was up to him, and that meant he was dead meat.

He pushed his glasses back up his nose and gave the only acceptable excuse he could think of. "I . . . my mom made me wear them."

The boys hooted with laughter.

"Mommy made *Dickie* wear his white socks!" Billy pursed his lips, making kissy noises.

Richard fought back the twin urges to hit and to cry. The first would get him killed, for sure, and the other would make things worse than ever. He wished he were like one of the Monkees on TV. Those guys could say anything and do anything, and be cool. Or he'd like to be one of the Beatles. Or Steve McQueen, jumping over them on his motorcycle in a great escape. Yeah, McQueen was the coolest guy ever. He bet if

Steve wore white socks, no one would say a word. Movies and TV were his friends, a place to hide and be somebody else.

But he knew he wouldn't turn into a miracle of coolness. He'd always be skinny and weak with glasses, big clunky teeth, and super-wavy hair that had to be plastered down or it looked as if he'd stuck his finger in an electric socket. He didn't know why he never said the right things; he just never did. And his face turned beet red every time he opened his mouth.

He'd *told* his mother he couldn't wear white socks, but she had only laughed. She never understood about clothes. He bet that his brother's hand-me-down plaid flannel shirt was next on Billy's lists of torments. It wasn't. Instead, Billy reached out and snatched his glasses off his nose. Richard yelped and grabbed for them, knowing his parents would murder him if anything happened to the glasses. His stomach clenched with fear as Billy threw them to one of his friends. A game of catch began. The world now a fuzzy blur, Richard didn't have a hope of catching those glasses.

"Give 'em back!" he shouted, sniffling back tears of frustration.

"Okay," Billy said, and threw the glasses directly at him.

To Richard's horror, they bounced off his chest and sailed over the heads of the boys surrounding him. His only thought was to catch them before they hit concrete, so he broke through the ranks of boys and ran down the steps.

A little girl was standing on the grass, shyly holding something out to him. Richard squinted as he neared and saw his glasses in her hand. By some miracle they weren't broken, not even a lens cracked. They must have landed on the grass ... or the phantom of Steve McQueen had caught them in his famous baseball glove.

"Thanks," he said gratefully, taking the glasses from her and putting them on.

An older girl came up, looked at him as if he'd grown a horn in the middle of his head, then pushed the younger one away. "Come on, Penny! Geez, you dumb kid, do I have to tell you everything?"

Now that he could see, he found that the rescuer of his glasses was chubby and small enough to be a kindergartner. She had a shock of red hair that tangled wildly about her head and a face covered with freckles. She was even uglier than he. Recognition rose up inside him, and he felt sorry for her. The kid was just starting out, and she probably had no idea what was in store for her.

He wasn't about to tell her.

ONE

"Miss? Are you lost?"

Pen Marsh turned at the sudden sound of the man's voice behind her in the woods. Her heart thumped painfully with fear, then with something else entirely as she got a glimpse of the magically appearing vision. Magic it was, because he hadn't been there a second before—and no modern man looked like he did.

She gaped like a teenager. He was tall and lithe, with long arms and legs, and the compact and defined muscles of an Olympic diver. His face could have been carved in stone for all the expression it gave off, including the little half-smile hovering around his lips. But his eyes . . . it was as if all his emotions were stored in them. Keen intelligence and humor gleamed out of the leaf-green depths. She knew women who would kill for that color—and for his hair. Really, she thought, nothing was more depressing than to see a man with thick, wavy, luxurious locks hanging to his shoulder blades. The front was pulled back off his face, but Pen had no doubt that let loose, his hair would frame his face naturally in a way that women spent hundreds of dollars to have a man named Mr. Raoul achieve for them. His forearms were corded like a ball player's, and tattooed with dots in intricate and intriguing patterns. Sure, quiet confidence shone out of him.

But his clothes marked him as coming from another time entirely. He wore a loose linen shirt held together by a beaded belt. Below were buckskin leggings that didn't quite reach the shirt, leaving a gap at his hips. Modesty prevailed with a loincloth. Pen couldn't help wondering if it hurt not to wear jockey shorts.

She dragged her gaze from that particular part of his anatomy and focused instead on the long rifle he cradled in his arms like a baby. In that instant the man glanced up sharply to his right, his rifle coming into his hands immediately. Pen turned, too, and saw an Indian standing on the ridge above. The top front of his head was shaved; the sides and back grew long and hung to his shoulders. No jeans and T-shirt for him either; this man wore only a loincloth and held a lethal-looking tomahawk in his hand.

"Hey, Creighton! Libby says haul your butt up here. It's time."

The man named Creighton waved in acknowledgment, then turned back to her. "Are you lost from your camp, miss?" he asked again. "These woods aren't safe for a woman alone."

Everything came together in that moment for Pen. Of course she knew who the man was and what he was doing here. She ought to. Her cousin, Libby Marsh, was directing a movie here at the Delaware Water Gap in New Jersey. It was about the colonial frontier, a "politically correct" movie, according to Libby, covering the founding of Fort Nashborough. Titled *American Saga*, the film starred Richard Creighton.

Richard Creighton had become a big star when he burst on the scene several years back, with a brilliant performance as an innocent pulled down by the big city before redeeming himself. But Pen knew this man from further back than the movies. *This* was the Cretin? Libby had said he'd changed, but she hadn't said how much.

"You're a mute, aren't you?" he asked gently, taking her elbow. "Come. Allow me to escort you to our camp until we can find your folks."

His hand was a sensual heat on her skin, bringing her awareness into suddenly sharper focus.

"Ahhh . . ." she said as her brain went instantly dead. It was the only part of her that wasn't working. Her senses were acute; her body was on fire.

He smiled at her. "Ezekiel Freemont, at your service. I assure you you're very safe with me. I'm known throughout the frontier for not hurting any creatures except redcoats, French and Spanish, and the occasional Chickasaw, enemies to my brothers, the Cherokee."

"Ahhh . . ." A fistlike pressure contracted her diaphragm, and she couldn't get air to her voice to speak.

"Don't strain yourself, miss," he said, nudging her into walking up the steep pathway. "Talking hurts the jaws at the best of times and the ears most of the rest."

Pen silently cursed herself. Why the hell wouldn't her voice work? All she had to say was "I'm Penelope Marsh, Pen's my nickname. I'm Libby Marsh's cousin, and I've been invited to the set to watch the filming." Simple words, not a one over three syllables. Instead, she sounded like a drooling idiot. She touched her chin just to be sure. It was dry. Taking heart, she finally managed to get some coherent words out.

"Omigod! You're Richard Creighton!"

He laughed, transforming the stony features into handsome warmth. "Never heard of the man, but lucky him if he knows a pretty woman like you."

Pen blinked. What did he mean he'd never heard of himself? And what did he mean that she was pretty? She was too tall—she was five feet nine in her stocking feet—wore a size ten on her fattest days, and had features that were nondescript even with full makeup. She saw herself in the mirror every day, so she ought to know. Worse, she saw herself against all the sweet young upscale things who attended Blair Academy.

They'd make a Miss America look ugly. Good thing the college was out for the summer, otherwise there would be big trouble. Movie crews and college girls didn't mix.

"I'm confused," she said finally, bringing herself back to the current crisis: her own stage fright.

"Ah, she speaks!" His smile turned into a grin. "Don't worry, we'll find your folks."

"But I'm not lost. . . ."

Her voice trailed away as they crested the hill. A meadow spread out before them. Trailers, lighting stands, cameras, microphone booms, and cables covered the ground. People milled around, half of them dressed in costumes of a time more than two hundred years in America's past. Several Indians in loincloths, bows slung across their backs, wicked-looking spears at their sides, were playing with portable video games near a wooden fort that had only two walls.

"Richard! Oh, good, you brought Pen up with you. I don't know if you remember Pen from grade school or not, but she probably remembers you." A woman, as short as Pen was tall and on the dieter's side of near plump, got out of a nearby director's chair. Libby Marsh, hurrying toward them, looked about as tough a Hollywood director as a Cabbage Patch doll, complete with curly red hair and freckles.

Pen hugged her cousin, grateful to find one piece of sanity in the insanity.

"Okay!" she yelled, clapping her hands for attention. "Those of you about to get killed, get into position. Indians, I want good war whoops this time. You all sounded like wounded ducks in that camp scene yesterday. These people are taking your land, remember? Be angry and exuberant, for heaven's sake! Richard, you go right through the center of them to Robertson. Remember, you're trying to save the man even though you're in love with his wife. Colonials, you're fighting for your lives and your settlements, so be determined and fierce. Conflict, conflict, conflict. And someone get the damn dogs ready behind the fort gates! I want this authentic. I only hope they know which Indians they're supposed to go after. Okay! Pen, take a seat and don't trip over anything. Everyone, just the way we rehearsed it. I want this in one take, otherwise we'll have to set up all over again. *So no one screw up!*"

Pen turned to thank Richard Creighton, determined to behave like the mature twenty-nine-year-old teacher of gifted students that she was. But what she found when she faced him had her gaping again.

His expression was closed and his eyes were cold as he stared at her. She felt his aloofness coming at her in waves, as if she'd offended or insulted him beyond forgiveness. She had no idea what she'd done or said to cause this reaction.

He inclined his head. "Miss."

Mystified, her heart sinking, Pen watched him go to play colonial cowboys and Indians.

—◆———◆—

Richard leaped over two men falling to their "deaths." He wondered if Pen Marsh remembered him from grade school. He "hit" an Indian with the stock of his rifle and ran full-tilt through the turmoil of fighting bodies. She must remember. He elbowed several people out of the way of his mad dash. Hadn't he been the butt of the school jokes back then? Who could forget Richard "Cretin"? An enemy rose up suddenly in front of him, screaming fiercely, his tomahawk raised. Richard blocked it with his forearm and "plunged" his knife into the man's stomach. He didn't wait for the man to cry out again and collapse into the dirt, but kept running. Even if she didn't remember, he thought, Libby had reminded her. That turned him cold. Robertson was just ahead of him, fighting off five Indians, using his Kentucky flintlock as a club since he didn't have time to reload. But the man was losing ground fast. In moments he'd be dead if he wasn't reached in time. Richard ran on while wondering why he should be so bothered by the question of whether or not Pen remembered him. He shoved several final men out of his way. She had been a surprise to him, he admitted it—

"Cut!"

A groan went up from the sweating men, who immediately broke from their fighting stances. The "dead" ones rose like a troop of Lazaruses. Richard stopped mid-stride, bewildered out of his trance. He wondered who screwed up the scene.

Libby got out of her director's chair and came over. To him. "Richard. Angel. The moves look good, but you don't seem to be with the program. . . ."

Richard could feel his face heating up as Libby ticked off everything that had been off in his performance in the scene. He glanced over at Pen. She was staring at him. He cursed himself for even looking at her, let alone checking her reaction. She had attracted him from his first sight of her in the forest, and he had tracked her through the woods like a schoolboy. Then he'd hidden behind the facade of the character he was playing in this film. It had seemed easier. It always did. Besides, he had been in the midst of preparing himself for the scene, and it was a way to keep in character, or so he'd rationalized. Silly. And worse, he was being dressed down in front of her.

He didn't intend to tolerate it any longer.

"Look, Libby," he interrupted, "I did the scene as choreographed, directed, and rehearsed. Don't tell me I didn't."

Libby eyed him. The silence on the set was deafening as the star disagreed with the director. Everyone waited with bated breath to see who would win control. The first week always set the tone for the rest of the shoot, and Richard knew he had put his director in an untenable position. He respected his directors, and he respected Libby more than most. She didn't shred an actor's ego; she coaxed a performance out of him or her.

He hadn't been in the head of his character, Ezekiel, and he knew it. Furthermore, Libby knew it. He'd totally lost concentration. It was the first time he had let it happen in his career.

"You're right, though," he said. "My mind was . . . elsewhere." He forced himself not to glance at the reason. For a passive observer, she caused a lot of commotion—inside him. He added, "I wasn't in character, and I'm sorry."

Libby looked nonplussed for a moment, then grinned. Richard glanced at Pen. She was smiling, admiration in her eyes. He hoped. At least she wasn't looking at him as if he were the latest ogre out of Hollywood.

"Get your fanny in character, kid," Libby said. "Or I'll get Gibson or Costner."

Richard smiled. "And what you'd have is Gibson or Costner, not Ezekiel Freemont, and you know it. Those guys haven't had to act for years."

She chuckled. "Stinker. Okay, setup time again. Hold the dogs! Everyone might as well break for lunch." She glanced at her watch as she walked away. "Lunch at nine in the morning."

"Sorry, people," Richard called out. "Lunch is on me."

Everyone laughed. Full meals and snacks were provided by a company hired by the production company. But Richard knew his jest had helped restore good humor to the set. Libby was firmly in control of her movie and star again. Now he'd be able to fight for things that he felt were important without being perceived as difficult. The more one paid attention to the politics on a movie set, the more one was able to accomplish.

He realized he was in the middle of the location with only a few technicians, who were resetting the scene. Well, he thought, he was living up to his old nickname, standing here like an idiot. He wasn't ready to go into his trailer yet. The spring day was beautiful, and he wanted to enjoy it.

Pen was still sitting in the chair Libby had directed her to. She looked out of place, uncomfortably so.

As he neared her, a variety of emotions rose up inside him, shutting off any thoughts of easiness with her. He wouldn't embarrass himself again. Besides, he was here to do a job, and he'd already screwed up once because of her.

Okay, so she was lovely, her slender body looking delectable in pink-and-white-striped shirt and jeans. She had legs that went on forever. Other men might call her skinny, but he considered her willowy. Her hair was a rich red, like leaves turned in the autumn chill; it was held back from her face by a pink bow, and her eyes were vivid blue. Any freckles she might have had were blurred by maturity into creamy skin. She wasn't beautiful. He'd seen his share of beautiful women who left a lot to be desired.

"I thought you were very good," she said when he passed close to her.

He paused. "You did?"

"It was amazing," she added enthusiastically, "how all of you did that without a single person being hurt. It looked so real when that man was ready to tomahawk you that I almost screamed. Only the thought of Libby killing me for messing up her scene kept me quiet."

He nodded again, not knowing what to say. He could smell the perfume she wore. It was light and fresh, like the scent of wildflowers on a dewy morning.

"I helped Libby find the locations here," she added, smiling at him. "It's really something to see all she talked about finally coming to life. Although I'm not sure why you're filming a movie based on the settling of Fort Nashborough, Tennessee, in northern New Jersey. I never have understood why movies aren't filmed in the places where they are set."

He smiled slightly. "Nashville, Tennessee, doesn't have the same geography as it had two hundred years ago, the same woodland area. And it's too built up where the story actually takes place. It happens a fair amount of the time when authenticity comes up against real life."

"I *see*." She grinned at him. "I've been babbling like an idiot, haven't I?"

"No . . . uh . . . no." He became aware of a breeze fluttering along his legs, picking up the ends of his loincloth. His hair was hanging heavy on his neck, reminding him of how strange he must look to her. His stomach knotted. His heart pounded faster. He couldn't seem to get his tongue working all of a sudden, a phenomenon left over from his painful childhood shyness. It usually struck at the worst times. This was one of them.

"I teach gifted students at the elementary school here," she was saying, "and my kids would just love this. Blairstown is pretty small and rural—"

"Excuse me," he blurted out, his voice working at last. He turned and strode off to the woods, his legs eating up the ground in an ever-quickening pace.

The green canopy of trees closed over his head, filtering the sun into pinpoint shafts of brilliance. He walked deeper into the bracken until the sounds faded behind him. His heart rate slowed to normal; his panic attack was subsiding.

He glanced down at his open shirt and loincloth and cursed the story line that dictated the costume. His profession always managed to ensure that no actor ever looked like a normal human being. He could just imagine what Pen Marsh thought of half his backside hanging out for the world to see. That she kept a straight face was a testament to her manners.

Manners made him think of his own. He knew he'd been abrupt with her, but her presence had thrown him back in time to his childhood. It seemed that he hadn't overcome as much as he thought.

"It's just a momentary throwback," he muttered. He had long ago determined he'd prove his worth to all those who'd maligned him. That was why he had never changed his name, something actors still did on a regular basis.

Taking a deep breath, he reminded himself he was here to do a job. And he'd do a damn good one and let the work speak for him. To everyone—especially Pen Marsh.

Now it was time to get into Ezekiel's skin once more.

He pushed on deeper into the woods.

Pen sat in a high canvas chair and watched the preparation for the reshoot of the battle sequence.

She wanted desperately to leave, feeling like a complete fifth wheel. Occasionally a member of the crew would look at her as if she were an annoyance, which she probably was, to be tolerated only because she was the director's relative, which she definitely was. Libby was off conferring with people and had no time to babysit her. And she had somehow offended the star.

She knew what she'd done with Richard—gone on like a giggly teenager and wasted his valuable time. He had tolerated all he could before excusing himself. He had given her plenty of signals that he needed to move on, not looking at her directly after their initial contact, for one. But, no, she'd gawked again, completely star-struck. How Libby even noticed he wasn't all there during the scene was unfathomable to her.

The man himself had been incredible, running and leaping and dodging in a way that Davy Crockett would have envied. So what if he'd had a faraway look in his eyes? His facial expression looked determined enough to her—more than determined. Lord, but she would love to have a man look at her that way.

"They leave you all alone, miss? Don't mind them too much. I doubt they'd pay attention to old Georgie himself if he showed up around here."

Pen turned around to find Richard behind her, grinning good-naturedly at her. He was leaning on his rifle, his forearms folded over the muzzle, the very picture of sexy and self-confident ease. Her heart seemed to stop beating, then pounded hard and fast.

"'Course if old George showed up in these parts, we'd probably shoot him for trespassing," Richard added. "I'd be first in line. Miss, you might want to close that pretty mouth of yours. Catching flies is a championship sport out here, but we tend to use our hands for it."

Pen could feel her jaw down somewhere around her knees. She closed her mouth, her face heating with embarrassment. She was doing it again, and she couldn't stop it. Come on, girl, she admonished. He puts his pants on one leg at a time. . . .

The images her fertile mind conjured had her almost gaping again. Damn, but the man was sexy. She coughed and cleared her throat. "It's okay. Everyone's busy—"

"Make-work. That's the problem with people nowadays," he said. "They put more elbow grease into make-work than into enjoying life. Give me a tent and a good hunting ground, and a man can live out his days in contentment."

"I . . . see." She didn't, but she wasn't about to admit it. He was talking to her again. A bit oddly, but talking. She wished she could grasp what he was saying, but they seemed somehow out of sync. Who was "George"? The former president? She didn't think he'd referred to George Bush.

He grinned. "You don't see, do you? Not until you live out there for a while, taking in beauty the way nature planned it."

Pen remembered Libby saying something about the studio sending Richard on a survival course before the movie. That must be what he was talking about. She tried for her best schoolteacher tone. Anything was better than stammering like a star-struck dolt. "I bet it was fascinating to learn all those woodsman's skills—"

"Necessary if a man wants to eat on a regular basis." He pointed to Libby. "Now there's a bossy woman. She'd probably tell General Washington he was crossing the Delaware the wrong way."

Pen chuckled, knowing Libby wouldn't even hesitate. "I'd hate to see what she would have told Patton."

"Don't know the gentleman, but I expect she'd give him an earful. But she's what the frontier needs. Not those prissy things we get now, all trussed up like turkeys ready for the spit." He turned to her, taking in her jeans and shirt. "You dress in a practical way, miss. I've seen a few women out here dress like a man. It makes sense to me, for what we're all doing."

It dawned on Pen that she wasn't talking to Richard Creighton, but to the character he played in this film. Old Georgie was not George Bush, but King George III. Of course Ezekiel wouldn't know who Patton was. Was this normal for actors to walk around in character when the cameras weren't rolling? Whatever, he was certainly charming and flirtatious now. He also might have a few screws loose. She pushed down her confusion. The man talked about enjoying life, so she certainly ought to enjoy this.

"Okay, everybody, we're ready for Take Two!" Libby shouted. "And only Take Two, Richard!"

Richard laughed. "See what I mean? Bossy."

Pen nodded.

"Wish me good luck, miss," he said, patting her on the back in a brotherly fashion. "I'm about to save a man I hate for the woman I love. Pardon my language, but honor is hell."

Pen's heart took several double beats before calming to its regular rhythm again. Or as regular as it was going to get around Richard Creighton.

The actors took position again on the "battlefield." Libby called for the action to begin. Pen watched in awe as "Ezekiel Freemont" outran, outshot, and outdodged death at every turn. The expression on his face was a frozen mask of resignation and sometimes of pain as the man did what he had to do in order to live with himself afterward.

If she thought she'd been star-struck before, she knew now she hadn't even been close.

What a man!

TWO

Libby's idea of a dinner party for twelve was three boxes of pizza, a case of soft drinks, no veggies and no dessert.

Pen grinned in amusement at her cousin as she managed to get a slice of plain cheese. The rest of the boxes' contents went in a swoop of hands. Every available chair was occupied, as was most of the floor space in the small living room of Libby's rented house. Pen had settled herself into a corner, a little out of the circle.

"Where's Richard?" someone asked.

The sixty-four-thousand-dollar question, Pen thought. She'd been up to the set every day for the past several days, watching them film. Richard hadn't done more than mumble a greeting to her. She had to admit she hadn't said much either, terrified she'd sound like an idiot again. But she'd come for dinner, knowing he was invited. Now she felt out of her depth in this mix of actors and technicians. They had talked business from the moment they'd walked in the door, most of it Greek to her. She still wasn't sure what a "best boy" was, but she did know the man they referred to was fifty if he was a day.

"He was supposed to be here," Libby said finally, looking around as if just realizing dinner had started without one of her guests. "You know Richard. He's living up there on the mountaintop like Daniel Boone. With no clock, he could show up anytime. Or not at all."

"Method actors," a grizzled-looking man said, chuckling. "Hell, they keep us in business."

"Really?" Pen said, focusing on Libby's words. "He's living outdoors like a frontiersman?"

"It keeps him in character," Libby said. "Richard's fanatical about it. That's why he's so good, although it must be hell when it rains."

"And the mosquitoes," Pen murmured, knowing how nasty they got during New Jersey summers. It was no better here in the Kittatinny Mountains than it had been at her childhood home in the flat southern end of the state.

"Richard's probably swathed in mud or bear grease to ward them off," Libby said. "I didn't expect him to come, really. He's always been such a loner. You remember, Pen."

"Actually, I don't," Pen admitted. "You and he were years ahead of me in school. I was just a kindergartner, terrified of being away from my mother. You told me his family moved shortly after school started that year."

"Well, trust me, he was a loner." Libby laughed. "Who would have thought that Penns Grove, that little bitty town, could produce John Forsythe, Bruce Willis, Richard, and yours truly. How I got in there I'll never know."

Pen grinned. "Me neither."

Everyone laughed.

"Thanks. What a great relative you are." Libby munched on her pizza. "God, but I miss true pizza. The stuff we get in California is bread dough with sun-dried tomatoes and jack cheese. Easterners think they have died and gone to pizza hell."

"Here, here," half the group muttered, clearly Easterners missing their pizza with thin crust, overloaded with pungent oregano sauce and stringy mozzarella cheese.

"When's Mary Jane due in?" another person asked.

Pen knew the man was talking about the costar, Mary Jane Stevens, an actress with box-office draw. To her surprise, several expressions became closed. She wondered what the woman was like to cause such a reaction.

Libby shrugged. "We don't need her for a few

more weeks, and she has a conflict until then anyway."

The doorbell rang, and Pen knew immediately who it had to be. Abruptly she put down her slice of pizza, as on edge as a girl on her first date. She took a deep breath to calm herself as Libby went to answer the door. Five minutes with a famous actor, and she had become ridiculous in a full-fledged crush, with stars in her eyes and sludge in her brain. He had access to thousands of women, so why would one mundane schoolteacher interest him? Worse, even if the impossible happened and he was attracted to her, what on earth could she expect but to be left? He was only in town for a short time and then he'd be gone. She ought to remember that and start acting her age. She was a mature woman with several long-term relationships behind her, none of which panned out into marriage. She was damn grateful for that, she thought, since all three of the men with whom she'd been involved seemed to have had the Peter Pan syndrome. For some unfortunate reason, she'd been drawn to that kind of man. She thought she was past it, holding out now for a good guy or a terrorist, whichever came along first.

Richard Creigton had all the earmarks of a Peter Pan.

Dammit, she thought in disgust. She was quite content with her life. She was proud of her hard-won sense of self-worth, and gawking at famous actors was not her style!

Richard wasn't wearing any home cures for keeping the insects away. He had on normal jeans and a chambray shirt; his long hair was pulled back in a ponytail. His only concession to his character, if it was that, was the plain brown moccasins on his bare feet.

He looked sexier than ever.

Pen could feel her control slipping away and made a desperate mental grab for it. The man couldn't leap tall buildings in a single bound. He only looked that way.

A couple of people said hello, and Richard nodded in acknowledgment. Pen noticed he held his mouth tight, his chin almost rigid. It wasn't a look of anger, more like repression. He was famous, respected, and gorgeous, so she wondered what he had to be repressed about.

"I think there are a couple more slices left," Libby said, "if these pigs haven't eaten it all. Sit down over there by Pen."

In that instant Pen gladly would have shot her cousin. With a harpoon gun. To make matters worse, Richard sighed in clear disgust, yet dutifully stepped over a few bodies to get to a spot next to her. Pen edged over, giving him plenty of room. She smiled a hello. He nodded back.

Good job, Pen. She praised herself just as she would

one of her kids who had conquered a difficult problem. But even as she did, she became aware of the warmth of his body, the very maleness of him, separated from her by mere inches. Her heart thumped, her nerve endings sizzled, and her brain went blank. For a repressed guy, he oozed animal magnetism.

"How's it going up on the mountaintop?" Libby asked.

"Okay," Richard answered, and bit into his slice of pizza. "Good pizza."

"Come on, Richie," Libby coaxed. "Quit doing your Gary Cooper impression. Have you been fighting off any bears up there? Dancing with wolves? Kicking the you-know-what out of mutant woodchucks?"

Pen grinned at her cousin's teasing. Libby would be irreverent with the Pope, and Lord help them all if she ever got within speaking distance of the man.

"I had a run-in with a skunk this morning," Richard answered, chewing thoughtfully. "I named her Libby."

Everyone laughed. Libby said, "Hey, Bill, make a note. We're moving up to tomorrow the shoot where Richard's supposed to fall off the cliff into three feet of water and survive."

Richard chuckled. It had a rich, deep sound of genuine affection to it. Pen smiled in surprise and appreciation. She hadn't thought the real Richard had a sense of humor. Ezekiel, yes. Richard, no.

Then she wondered about her cousin, who had

drawn it out of this cold, silent man. What was Libby's relationship with him that she could do it? They were of an age and background, and Pen knew Libby was not long out of a painful divorce. Were she and Richard together?

An icy chill settled on her. The thought hurt worse than she cared to admit. She reminded herself to get a grip on her emotions and imagination. They could be whatever they wanted to be, and it shouldn't matter to her. She was just a standby observer for the summer.

She groaned. It was only June.

Forcing herself to act like the intelligent woman she'd thought she was, Pen said, "I can't thank all of you enough for your patience in putting up with me on the set. Libby's probably told you I teach science to gifted elementary school kids, and I want my students to learn how a movie is made. Can I ask you a few questions? On your breaks or something, of course, where they wouldn't be in the way."

"Thank God for that," Libby said. "I love you, but the thought of 20 eight-year-olds wandering the set gives me the shingles. 'School's out' never sounded sweeter."

"They'd be better behaved than you," Pen retorted, grinning.

Everyone hooted.

"Can she go over the cliff with Richard?" Libby asked the room in general. "It would be good pathos. And Pen would be great for the part."

"You'd be dead meat," Pen told her. She was aware of Richard listening intently and forced herself to turn and smile at him. "Hope you don't mind if I bow out of that."

"Not at all," he said. "I've told Libby she ought to get herself in front of the camera. Maybe this is the scene for you, Lib."

"It would turn into slapstick," Libby said. "Okay, I know when I've lost it."

"Why don't you make a videotape of our filming for your class?" Richard suggested. "I don't think any of us would mind. You could interview the cast and crew on what they do."

Pen knew a brilliant idea when she heard one, and immediately turned to her cousin. "Can I, Lib? I promise I won't get in the way. I can tape from the sidelines, then get interviews on your breaks. It would be a terrific opportunity—"

"Lord help me," Libby interrupted. She fixed a measuring stare on Pen, who smiled back innocently. Finally Libby sighed. "I suppose, although I ought to be strung up. 'Entertainment Tonight' would kill to get on this set, and I give a schoolteacher completely free rein. Oh well, what's a little nepotism between cousins?"

"Nepotism is when you *hire* your relatives," Pen said. "And you're not paying me, that's for sure. This, my ignorant cousin, is education for all the future filmmakers who come out of Blairstown, New Jersey."

"Who are going to grow up and knock me out of a job," Libby muttered, to everyone's amusement. Even Richard chuckled.

Pen turned to him and said, "Thank you for the suggestion. It's a wonderful one, and I think my students will learn a lot from a tape."

Richard nodded and bit into his pizza, mumbling, "Welcome."

Okay, Pen thought, she got his message. She waited about twenty minutes, staying out of the conversation, then gave her hands a last final rub with the paper napkin and rose to her feet, saying, "Thanks for the pizza, Libby, but it's late, and I really have to get going."

Libby started to protest. At Pen's best school-teacher, no-nonsense look, Libby changed direction and immediately stood up. "I understand. We're all used to the dawn-to-midnight schedule, but you're not. Besides, you have your own film to shoot."

Pen chuckled. "And I better figure out where I'm going to get a video camera by Monday. Good night, everyone."

There was a chorus of good nights. Even one from Richard. Well, Pen thought, a moment of civility. He wasn't hard to figure out. Even if she hadn't known something about his childhood, it would still be obvious he must have been a shy boy who had become a loner as an adult. Rudeness came to him unconsciously, Pen was sure. She was certain he didn't try to put off people deliberately. His profession was cutthroat, and he had probably been burned along the way by "friends." If he kept strangers at arm's length, no one could blame him.

"This was probably boring for you," Libby said when they reached the front door and were out of earshot of her other guests. "I'm sorry. I should have thought of that."

"Are you kidding?" Pen retorted. "Here I am, eating pizza with all you celebrities! I loved it. And I got a great idea for next year's class. Thanks for giving it the green light."

"The studio'll have my head, and probably the Directors' Guild too." With her wide grin, Libby didn't look worried. "I figure if I lose everything, I'll just move in with you."

Pen smiled. "In a pinch. It's been great to have you around."

"It has been."

Funny, Pen thought, once she was outside in the warm night air. She and Libby hadn't been close as children, even though they had both grown up in the same town and their fathers, the brothers, were close. It was sometime after college that their personalities seemed to have really clicked and they'd become friends.

She hadn't bothered to bring her car on such a beautiful night, Blairstown being small enough that Libby's house was about a five-minute walk from hers. She'd heard that some of the townspeople had rented their houses to actors and crew for exorbitant rates, then gone off to live elsewhere—many to the coastal resort towns—for the rest of the summer. So much for their panic of six months ago at the announcement of the selection of Blairstown as the site for filming. Blair Academy had offered up some of their dorm space to house the crew, since hotels were nonexistent and school would be out. Despite that, people had argued against the project, worried about how it would disrupt their lives. Now they were milking the experience for all it was worth. If the movie became a big success, she had no doubt there'd be signs going up everywhere that would say, "So-and-so slept here." George Washington would be envious.

She might as well enjoy her walk, before the town council turned the place into a tourist trap.

She became aware of the slap of feet behind her. People didn't hurry in Blairstown. Suddenly the quiet, safe street didn't seem so safe. She turned around, her muscles tensing. It was Richard.

"I saw you walking along in the direction I'm going," he said, halting several feet away from her under the lamplight. His face was half in shadow, his body in full light. "I hope I didn't scare you."

"Just a little." She smiled. "That's okay. I have an overactive imagination. One has to, to keep up with my students."

"Must be a real challenge keeping up with bright, energetic kids."

"It is. Hectic too," she said, beginning to walk again. His presence made her so nervous. The warm night was getting warmer as her body heated to the sight of Richard, looking so sexy, so strong.

He caught up alongside her. Pen told herself not to panic or be too pleased.

He added, "It's not good for a woman to walk alone at night."

"Here in Blairstown?" Blairstown was so sleepy, the sandman never bothered to stop.

"Even here."

He seemed firm about it. She decided not to argue. If Richard Creighton took it into his head to walk her home, to protect her, she was not about to say no.

Watch out, she warned herself. She could lose all her newfound "He's just a man" attitude with this one courtly gesture of his. Unfortunately, the rest of her had the urge to lap it up. "Thank you. That's very kind."

"Do you live close?" he asked.

"On the other side of town. Despite the college, we *are* talking major small town here," she added. "The place practically shuts down at the end of the school year. The area's all farms or wealthy homes, with the latter scattered up the mountains, the farms along Route 94. We may have a riding and hunt club, but that's more of a draw for the college students and their parents. Blair Academy is old money, but Blairstown is mom-and-pop. It's tinier than Penns

Grove ever was. Heck, we're even too small to be the town in the *Back to the Future* movies."

"Penns Grove was tiny," he admitted, smiling slightly. "If I remember correctly, it was just one part of a continuous strip of small towns down there that fed all its residents into the DuPont or Hercules chemical plants."

Pen grinned, glancing at him. "Your memory's right on. That part of the state was either 'Swamp or DuPont,' as my father likes to say."

"Was?" he asked.

She nodded. "It's changed some, with a lot of plants downsizing and some even closing. Penns Grove and Pennsville, next door, have grown a bit in spite of all that."

"Is that why you live up here?" he asked. "I'd think you'd be teaching school down there, especially if the town's grown a bit."

She grinned again, wryly this time. "Ah, but not if you take a degree in education along with fifty percent of the grads on a national basis during a three-year period. And all this at the same time as a slowdown in growth of the population of school-age children. Talk about a glut of teachers. The baby boomers had no one to teach. I was lucky to get anything in the state. But I like it here. I don't think I'm made for anything but small-town life."

Was she? Even as the words left her mouth, she wondered. Libby's life was very exciting, and she envied her cousin at times—especially when the kids acted up or the school board threatened to dismantle the special program because it was costly. Or when she was lonely.

He seemed to mull over her explanation as he walked beside her. Pen smiled as she turned corners and he followed. This was nice, she thought, even if she couldn't seem to tear her gaze away from him at times. And he did seem genuinely interested in her and the town. Though a doubting-Thomas voice reminded her that he was a very good actor.

The air was tinged with the scents of roses and male; the sharp contrast of sweet and musky enticing her senses. It was only pheromones, she told herself. Just those scents human bodies emitted to attract the opposite sex. Okay, so his pheromones were extraordinary. That didn't mean he liked her . . . was attracted to her as she was to him.

"I understand you're camping out up in the mountains," she said.

"I am," he agreed. "It puts me more in tune with Ezekiel, my character."

"You think of him as a real person, don't you?" she asked, trying to not to notice how close his body was as they passed along a house with a large boxwood hedge. Bare inches separated them. Pen resisted the urge to touch him and kiss him . . . kiss him until she knocked his socks off. She reminded herself he wasn't wearing any.

"I think you have to think of the character as a real person and become him to achieve a totally convincing performance."

For a moment she had no idea what he was talking about, then remembered her question. She cleared her throat, which had suddenly seemed to go dry on her. "That makes sense. Did you really name a skunk after Libby?"

He chuckled—a real one, just for her. It was a miracle, Pen thought.

"I did. It came up behind me this morning and just let go."

"You poor thing," Pen said, chuckling with him.

"Fortunately, it didn't get me directly. You know, Libby used to sneak up and let me have it when I went to your school. She was one of my tormentors."

Pen blinked at the surprising admission. "Really? But you get along so well now."

He snorted, a sound that easily conveyed his disgust and amusement. "She approached me several years back at a studio party and said, 'I went out of my way as a kid to torture you, and I'm sorry because I think you and I could make great movies together.' She was charming and hard to resist. Besides, I looked at it as coming full circle." He glanced at her. "You probably remember me from school."

"Actually, I don't," she said, repeating the words she'd used at the party. She almost related that, when it occurred to her he might be offended that he'd been talked about behind his back, no matter how innocent or favorable the remarks. "I was a gawky carrot-topped kindgergartner, scared to death I wouldn't make it through the school day without tossing my cookies." She laughed. "I still see a lot of kids like that."

He didn't laugh with her. Instead, he said, "I think I remember you. You picked up my glasses one day when Billy Prescott was throwing them around."

The name Billy Prescott rang a bell, but the incident didn't. She smiled, though. "I don't remember that. Maybe it wasn't me."

"I think so." He actually grinned. "It was the carrot-top that made me remember, because I recall how sorry I felt for you. I was sure you were next to get tormented."

She laughed, not quite as jovially as she would have liked. He had been more right than she cared to admit. "Junior high school was where I got it the worst. At five foot nine, I was taller than every boy by a head and my bright red hair seemed to shine like a beacon. My hair color has faded some, thank goodness. School dances were not my favorite recreation, needless to say. It wasn't until college that I developed an inordinate interest in the men's basketball team."

He laughed again. Boy, but was she on a roll, she thought. He said, "I bet the basketball team had an inordinate interest in you. I would have."

Pen's heart slowed as her breath caught and the stars seemed to spin around her. The sensation passed, but the words "I would have" lingered. She told herself not to be silly. It was a very nice compliment, and that was all it was. To cover her jangled state, she asked, "So where are the glasses now?"

"Contacts." He grinned. "I wonder what Billy would have done about them."

"Probably run for the hills," she muttered, thinking of the battle scene she'd witnessed the other day.

"I beg your pardon?"

"Nothing."

She realized they were on her street, nearly at her house, a small, narrow one which she liked very much. She pointed and said, "That's my house there. Thank you for walking me home. It was very kind of you."

"Just common sense." He seemed relaxed and easy with her. "I'll walk you to your door."

She wondered what the tabloids would say about Richard Creighton walking a schoolteacher to her door, then decided that was non-news for sure. Still, she'd dine out on it for a long time to come.

"So you were my rescuer that day," he said, as they reached her walk. "That was very gutsy of you. I can't remember if I thanked you or not."

She smiled. "Kids don't think about things like that. Besides, I don't remember." She shrugged and he leaned over and kissed her.

THREE

Her lips were warm silk, drawing him up in flames.

He hadn't wanted to go to Libby's pizza party, but he'd forced himself to, knowing it was good for relations with the crew. And knowing *she* would be there. Why Libby's cousin should attract him so was puzzling. He certainly hadn't understood it—or understood why he'd had an overwhelming urge to leave with her.

Now he did.

He pulled her to him, almost as roughly as the bolt of pure desire that shot through him. He gripped her upper arms, marveling at the feel of her flesh against his hands. Her breasts were pressed against his chest, her hips to his, inflaming him in an instant. His relationships with women had been few and far between, and none had ever caused such a swift and complete reaction. She made little noises in the back of her throat, and he plunged his tongue inside her mouth, seeking hers for a gentle duel. That she didn't respond in kind immediately penetrated his passion-fogged brain. He let her go.

To his surprise, *she* looked surprised, as if she had expected the kiss to continue. But by the outside light at the front door, he could see her lips were swollen and slightly bruised looking. He realized he hadn't been as careful with the kiss as he should have been. He cleared his throat to speak, but words failed him.

Pen smiled into the awkward silence and said, "Thanks for walking me home, Richard. And thanks for the idea about using the video camera. It was a terrific one."

"You're welcome," he began, trying to figure out how to express his feelings.

She got her door open before he could say anything. "Good night."

"Uh . . . good night," he said lamely. Suddenly he was staring at wooden panels.

He'd done better with Libby the skunk.

Two days later, Richard couldn't help noticing Pen on the set. Hand-held video camera practically glued to her right eye, she had been filming anything that moved for two days. People grinned at her and hammed it up for the camera, but he could feel her presence yet again penetrating his Ezekiel overlay.

He had opened himself to her the other night . . . the real him, when he'd only meant to draw her out instead. As with Libby, he found it hard to keep himself bottled up and not hide behind his character. Somehow she had her cousin's knack for pushing through barriers—but with a twist. He'd never had a twinge of desire for Libby. For Pen, his desire was growing monumentally. Each passing day he wanted her even more . . . until, he feared, the wanting would overwhelm him like a fierce storm. She wasn't for him, he thought. Women like Pen never were—and he'd been holed up in his camp, reminding himself of that fact.

She innocently added to his torture by wearing a light blue sleeveless dress with a scoop neckline. The hint of cleavage she displayed was enticing. The dress clung to her slender curves before falling into a slightly gathered skirt. He'd heard them called ballet dresses, although he wasn't sure why, but Pen certainly had the figure for them. Her hair glinted in the sun, seeming almost to have a life of its own, magical and beckoning. So vividly alive and sweetly lovable, Pen was driving him mad, absorbing his attention, concentration . . . caring.

Eventually, inevitably, the glowing black eye of her video camera trained itself on him. Behind it Pen's voice said, "How do you get into the part you're playing?"

"I don't talk to people with video cameras," he

snapped in exasperation as Ezekiel Freemont vanished only minutes before an important scene.

Pen immediately lowered the camera. "I'm sorry, Richard."

"It's okay. I just need privacy."

She smiled slightly. "Of course."

As she walked away he realized he'd offended her and wished for the easiness of the other night. That sort of relaxation never came naturally to him, but took weeks and months to achieve with people. He cursed himself and moved two steps after her to apologize, but was brought up short by Libby's voice.

"Okay, Indians and settlers, this is the signing of the peace treaty. I know it's hard to shoot out of sequence, but for lots of reasons we've got to get the denouement in the can now. Indians, it's the end of your way of life, the opening of the Western frontier to the white man, so remember you are to look defeated. Richard, you're an onlooker; you've come back after several years' absence. Charlotte, your great love, is not here, but her husband, James, is. I want this to be that final moment of pain for you personally. You've brought about the downfall of your own way of life as a 'Long Hunter.' It's gone now. We'll do close-ups on you. . . ."

Richard cursed again, knowing he was nowhere near emotionally ready to play this scene. But he took his position, focusing on his character's interior. Libby called for "action" and he looked on the scene before him, watching James Robertson, the fort's cofounder, make a final peace with the tribes. Dammit, he thought, why couldn't he have found the right words for Pen just now—

"Cut!"

"I know, I know," Richard called out in disgust. "I'm not in the right emotional state."

Libby shared a grin with the continuity director standing beside her. "Actually, Jim here has the ear plugs for his Walkman sticking out of his loincloth. Research didn't say that the Chickasaws had them in the eighteenth century."

Everyone roared with laughter over the star being caught out.

Richard knew a moment of embarrassment, then he noticed Pen smiling at him, and he smiled briefly back at her before turning his attention to his work. He'd been granted a reprieve, and he intended to take advantage of it, pulling up all the nuances that Ezekiel would feel. As the cameras rolled once more, he kept his gaze focused on the principals of the treaty while his mind was filled with the woman he could never have and would leave behind with another man.

"Cut! Perfect!"

Richard came out of his fog to find Libby grinning at him. "It looks great. Let's get set for the retake. Just a few notes for you . . ." Libby launched into directions to the cast.

They ran through the scene again, and again Libby

was satisfied with it. During the next setup, Richard knew he had to do something and strode right over to Pen.

"Here, miss," he said, forcing an Ezekiel grin. "I believe you asked a question earlier about my character. I wouldn't be honest if I didn't say my character has a blemish or two, but Ezekiel Freemont's word is his bond."

The video camera was up, the red light lit.

His grin widened. "Can't say I ever saw a pair of specs like that, although I heard tell Master Franklin's are a wonder, as are most of his inventions."

Pen laughed. "So I've heard. How do you play someone from two hundred years in the past?"

"Very carefully." He leaned on his rifle.

"What would you shoot with your rifle?"

"Mostly bad men and good buffalo. Seems a shame, doesn't it, to have to shoot the good ones, too, just to eat? You would have thought the Good Lord would have been more efficient about the process."

"Buffalo? Have you been out west?"

"You can't get much farther west than this!" He grinned. "Buffalo's plentiful here in the Transylvania Territory, although I have heard it's called Tennessee."

"But buffalo . . . oh, you mean *at this time.*"

"Yep. One beast can keep a family warm and full for an entire winter."

Pen's questions went on, and he answered them in the spirit of his character. Finally she put the camera away and said, "You were wonderful, Richard. The children will love it."

He smiled at her, grateful she seemed to have forgiven him. But he still had something to say. "I'm sorry about earlier. I was unfair."

She shook her head. "No. I was being an annoyance. And after I promised not to . . . am I keeping you from anything? Your preparation time? Rest time? Whatever you do with your off-time because I don't know what actors do with their extra time?"

"Mostly be bored," he said. "And no, you're not keeping me from anything. Actually, you kept me in the 'mode.' I told you before that I find it's better if I really throw myself into a role. Weeks ahead of rehearsals I start to get right into his skin and live him. Most people think I'm a nut." He shrugged. "But that's what works for me."

"Can you repeat that exactly?" Pen asked, bringing the camera back up to her eye.

He laughed. "You're as bad as Libby."

"No, no, not that." But the camera stayed trained on him.

"There is a family resemblance, trust me." He snorted in amusement and talked about his method of preparing for a role. "I've noticed you're filming everything all the time. Do you have a storyboard?"

Pen lifted her head and looked directly at him. "A what?"

"A storyboard. It's like a game plan. You decide overall what your story is, how to tell it logically, what you want to film for each scene, and who you need in the scenes. Why do you wear your hair back in that ponytail?"

She blinked, then touched her hair. "It's hot today."

He nodded, not saying more. Instead, he found his gaze focusing on her dress again. Her long legs were bare of stockings, yet just as smooth as any silk lingerie would make them. Very few American women wore dresses anymore in casual situations—or even formal ones. He was glad Pen was one of them. Very glad. He knew exactly what Ezekiel would say to her, so he said it.

"You look like the icing on a cake. Makes a man want to eat you up."

She blushed to the roots of her hair, and he chuckled, knowing she'd taken his words as risqué. He was finding he didn't mind that at all.

"I hate to break up this twosome," Libby said. Pen's blush became even rosier. "But the film's publicist is having a fit about you giving Pen an interview."

Richard glanced over at the man, who was glaring at them. "Why?"

"He says it's not fair that you won't give an interview to any of the entertainment shows and media people during the filming, but you give one to my cousin. He's moaning about your contract and that he has some say about who interviews you. He points out that Pen could even sell her tape with you to 'Entertainment Tonight' or something—"

"I wouldn't!" Pen gasped.

"Insulting women's honor is a poor sport for a man," Richard commented. He hefted his rifle upright, then unstoppered his powder horn and poured some of the black grains down the bore of the long steel barrel. He leisurely pulled out a musket ball from his pouch, tore off a piece of cloth from the rag he carried and wrapped it around the ball, then used a slender ramrod to push it down the bore until it could be pushed no farther. He set the rifle against his shoulder, peering down the sights. They were set straight at the publicist, who suddenly paled and froze in place.

"A fine rifle this," Richard told the women, keeping his eye on his target. "You can kill a varmint from two hundred yards and put the ball right in his nerdy pen pouch. I hope you are getting this on tape, Pen."

"From the moment you whipped out your thingie and started pouring your stuff down the hole."

The rifle went wide as Richard burst into laughter at her accidental double entrendre. Luckily for the publicist, the weapon didn't have a lit wick. Then he started laughing again as he wondered what Pen would have made of that fact.

"If Richard ever whipped out his 'thingie,' Pen, the ratings people would be down on us like flies on honey," Libby said, also laughing. "Not to mention his fans."

"I'd blush, but I don't think there's any more room left on my face," Pen said, looking heavenward for help. "I forgot what that damn thing—powder horn—was called for a moment, okay?"

"I wish I could see your students' faces when they see this part of the tape," Richard said. "If I had trouble with Ezekiel before, every time I have to load this rifle, I'll be a goner."

Libby made a face. "Lord help me on all those outtakes. What do you want me to tell the publicist?"

Richard smiled coldly. "He's welcome to fuss with the producer over the terms of my contract, and if they're that unhappy that I've broken any clauses, they're welcome to replace me."

"Oh, boy," Pen said.

Libby just smiled. "He'll stroke on the spot."

"So call an ambulance. And call me when you're ready to shoot the next scene." Richard grabbed Pen by the arm and stalked away.

"Uh . . . Richard?" Pen began.

"Yes? What?" He kept them moving away from the set and toward the woods.

"Maybe you shouldn't be so mad at the publicist. It wasn't fair to him that I was making a—"

"I'm not here to worry about a publicist," Richard snapped. "I make sure I do my job in front of the cameras so the crew can do theirs. Those people would have media all over a set if they could." He glanced over at her. "And you're not doing anything wrong, okay?"

"Okay." She grinned. "Since I'm not doing anything wrong, why are we running away?"

"We're not running away. I want some privacy."

"Might as well be in for a lion as for a lamb. Since you're going for some privacy and taking me along, how about an interview for my kids? And a real rifle demonstration?"

He laughed. "You *are* as bad as Libby."

Pen smiled as Richard, in full regalia, explained for the camera how to follow tracks and stalk a deer or a rabbit by the wood signs they left. He'd already done a second demo of loading the rifle, with no contemplated human target this time, and given a thorough description of his clothing and his arm tattoos, which turned out to be a temporary ink he got off with nail polish remover.

He was wonderful, and she was already half in love with him.

The thought pulled her abruptly upright.

"What?" Richard asked, staring up at her from his crouched position.

"Nothing." The word was little more than a croak. She cleared her give-away throat and fit the viewing piece back against her eye. When the "on" button showed red, Richard again began his explanation on how to part bushes without disturbing any occupants.

Silly, she thought, watching him in miniaturized black and white. She was just a little star-struck, not really half in love with him. She was a mature woman, and she wasn't a person to go gaga over a man. She wasn't gaga now. And she was smart enough to know that Richard had hundreds of beautiful women to choose from. Even if he had any interest in her, it was out of loneliness, nothing more. In the end he would want someone far prettier, more sophisticated, and more savvy on his arm at Hollywood premieres. He might look good in a loincloth, but fairy tales had little to do with real life. She had to keep her head screwed on straight and focused on *very* real life.

And if nothing else would do the trick, she ought to remember that kiss.

It had been swift . . . and awkward, a mashing of lips rather than a meshing. Granted, he had taken her by surprise, but it was more like the kiss of a young teenager. She would have thought his kiss would have caused all kinds of sparks to fly.

"If you're off in never-never land, you're in the wrong movie."

Pen blinked and straightened, letting the camera drop to her side. Richard was smiling in amusement at her. She cleared her throat. "Sorry."

He stepped toward her. "Stop apologizing so much."

"Sorry—" She chuckled. "I was born apologizing, I think."

"Well, stop now. It was the best advice I ever got."

He was so close to her, yet he didn't touch her. Frissons of awareness skittered along Pen's nerve endings. The air seemed to disappear from her lungs. Why, she wondered, had she ever thought she'd had no reaction to him? She was having a biggie this time. An eight on the Richter scale.

His lips settled on hers in an easy kiss, their mouths fitting together as if made for each other. Her eyelids fluttered closed. He kissed her so softly, with so little movement, that she wondered if he was unsure of his reception. She was aware of the video camera hitting the ground with a dull, safe thud as she stepped closer, pressing her body to his. Even as their lips parted by mutual unspoken consent, his breath, deep and quickening, brushed her ear. Then he kissed her again. His tongue swirled with hers, so much more gentle than the first time he'd kissed her. He had his passion in check. This, she thought dimly, was more like it. . . .

Suddenly he grabbed her against him, bending her back in Rudolph Valentino style.

"Richard," she gasped out. "My back!"

He straightened immediately, letting go of her. "I'm sorry, Pen . . ."

She chuckled. "Now who's apologizing?"

He didn't laugh, and she immediately sensed his embarrassment. His sudden reaction hadn't been from not caring for her feelings, otherwise why would he be embarrassed? He was shy, she knew that. But was he shyer and less experienced around women than she'd imagined? The notion was intriguing. She realized a more pressing need, however. He'd close her out again if she didn't bring him back right now.

"I didn't say stop," she said in a low voice, coming forward. She knotted her hands in the front of his linen shirt and leaned up and kissed him. The surprise on his face was so endearing that she had to grin. Maybe he just needed a little help, so she said, "Could we do that again? Only slower this time. I've never been kissed by a movie star before, and I want to savor the moment."

"Uh . . ." he began, clearly trying to find the words for a reason. She didn't want reason. She only wanted a kiss to remember, and pulled him down to her.

This kiss was everything she wanted, soft and filled with longing. Their mouths definitely fit together, and their tongues swirled and dueled and darted, the passion rising and spilling over in mutual satisfaction. The kiss turned hot, like molten lava on a reckless course down a mountainside. Her internal Richter scale went right off the chart, and what had before been one-sided now became a matching hunger. His scent permeated her senses. His skin was warm, almost burning to the touch. Her breasts were pressed against the solid wall of his chest, her hips to his. She could feel his legs braced slightly apart to take her weight, his hard thigh between her legs. His desire was obvious, and to her feminine satisfaction, completely for her. She plunged her fingers into his long hair, the strands coarser than her own, yet still surprisingly silky in their texture. She had never given a man with long hair a thought before, and now she'd never look at them the same again.

Her head was spinning when his mouth finally eased away from hers. He seemed to be holding her upright; her legs had turned to jelly.

She forced herself to open her eyes. His cheek-bones were stained with color, and his breath whistled harshly in and out of his lungs. But the expression on his face revealed smug satisfaction at her reaction to the kiss.

"That was some interview," she murmured.

He chuckled. "Do you get it all on tape?"

"What tape?"

"That's what I thought. Can I kiss you again?"

"Oh, boy," she muttered, and pulled his mouth down to hers.

When the call came for filming to resume, Pen had to admit it had been very pleasurable to have Richard all to herself—but for too short a time. *Very pleasurable.* The man could kiss the wings off an angel when he put his mind to it.

She reminded herself that great kisses do not a relationship make. And any relationship with Richard was really, in the end, futile. Actors and ordinary people did not mix. But she'd been thoroughly kissed by one of Hollywood's stars. That was more than enough for anyone's fantasy.

The scene called for Richard to be captured and tortured while on a scouting expedition, a far cry from the earlier one of the peace treaty. The filming was set up closer to the edge of the clearing, along a line of trees. Pen realized that no one viewing the final product would even know the two different scenes were being filmed in virtually the same spot. She noticed the publicist glaring at her with killer looks, but she kept herself well out of his way.

After Makeup finally stopped fussing over Richard, Libby explained again what she wanted from the actors. Everything went quiet. The film began to roll, and Richard began to step, with great care, beyond the tree line.

To Pen's horror, he was suddenly grabbed from behind, a tomahawk slicing down wickedly in front of his face, just before he flipped the Indian over his shoulder. He fought off several more and was slammed back brutally against a tree trunk, his arms bent behind him. He cursed, bucked, and fought to no avail; beads of sweat from pain ran down from his temples. The Indians whooped in victory. One of them took out a razor-sharp knife. He smiled at Richard, who stared stoically back. He ran the blade along Richard's arm. A thin line of blood appeared.

Pen gasped, then clamped her hands over her mouth.

Another cut appeared, and another, and another, on and on. . . .

"Cut!" Libby shouted finally. "Okay, let's get the blood up here, people."

Pen blinked out of her daze. Richard was released, laughing ruefully with his "captors" as he rubbed his upper arms. Makeup went to work on him to expertly transform him into a mass of bleeding cuts now. Get the blood up here, indeed! He already looked like the poster boy for a Band-Aid campaign. It took Pen a few moments to figure how the trick had been accomplished: Makeup had glued patches along his arms that, when cut open, simulated bleeding.

"Okay! Ready!" Libby yelled, bringing everyone back into focus.

The torture went directly to its last stages, when Richard was duly rescued by some of the settlers and carried out of the camera's view. Libby yelled "Cut" again.

Richard was unceremoniously dumped onto the ground and helped up by his dumpers, all of them laughing. Even Richard, the solemn man of a week ago, was smiling indulgently, as if to encourage their fun. She realized that he had good people skills, not dominating through demands or intimidation, but through recognizing the rites of passage a group of people working together required. It was rather like the classroom, where a teacher had to allow a certain amount of freedom or the children would clam up and be lost to her.

She realized then that Richard Creighton was already lost to her. He was from a world so entirely different from her own that there would never be any common ground between them. He might be a shy man, but this world was what he wanted. And it was not what she wanted.

Pen took a deep, painful breath, turned, and walked away.

FOUR

It took Richard several days to realize that Pen was evading him on the set. He watched her now, videotaping the best boy and grip as they explained their jobs with the set's electricals. She'd taped just about every member of the crew, including the caterer, but she hadn't taped him again.

He wondered if he was paranoid, or worse, having prima-donna-itis. He resented her paying attention to others. But why was she avoiding him? She tended to sit or stand by Libby or way off to the side of the filming area during breaks. If he was in one area, she always seemed to be in another. He'd joined her conversations with others several times, something he hated doing, never being quite sure of his reception. When the conversations faded naturally, she would excuse herself. He'd taken a while to catch on, but now he had.

He frowned as he turned away and tried to focus on his upcoming scene. What had he done to offend her? It was a question he'd asked himself over and over again. He thought he could pinpoint when it had happened. One moment they were kissing each other as if they were the only man and woman left on the earth, and the next moment she'd vanished. Right after that torture scene, in fact. But he couldn't pinpoint why. Maybe she'd been satisfied by that one kiss. Maybe she'd discovered too much about the real him.

He swung his gaze back to her and knew the real him wasn't so bad. He'd found people on this set, as on others in the past, liked him when he met them halfway. He'd even taken to not going off on his own during breaks but just hanging around, watching, although that was leading to another problem—Pen. Right now she was his concern. The easiest path he could take would be to let her go. But he knew he couldn't. Whatever it was that had frightened her off, he intended to find out. He picked up his ever-present rifle and started to walk toward her.

"Richard!" Libby called out. "We're ready for you."

Richard cursed under his breath at the bad timing, spun around, and went off to do his scene. He hated to delay dealing with the problem with Pen.

That evening he was on her doorstep. She'd disappeared again while he was filming. Angry and determined to have an honest confrontation, he knocked sharply on her door.

But the moment she opened it and a stricken look appeared in her eyes, he sensed that clearing the air would result in disaster.

"Hi," he said cheerfully, trying not to react to the allure of the flowing garment she wore. Although the cool material was voluminous, it somehow managed to reveal her curves in a softly enticing manner. One thing the outfit told him was that she hadn't been expecting company.

"Hi," she responded warily. "What are you doing here?"

The question was an ego deflator if he'd ever heard one. He grimaced, then forced a grin and said, "I thought I'd take you to dinner if you were free."

"Uh . . . well . . . I . . . uh . . . I'm making my own dinner. I mean, it's on the stove right now."

Bob Newhart didn't stammer nearly as well, Richard thought in disgust. Normally he would walk away at this point, but he sensed her evasion was a form of protection, not reluctance. The notion buoyed him, and he asked, "Got enough for two? I'm sick of barbecued hot dogs."

A chuckle escaped her. "Is that what you're eating up there? I had these visions of you catching and cooking Bugs Bunny or Bambi."

"Are you kidding? I'd starve to death." He smiled back. "So will you take pity on a poor starving actor and invite him in to share your dinner?"

A myriad of expressions crossed her face, all of them telling. At least they told him he had put her on the horns of a dilemma. Part of him wanted to say forget it and walk away, but he was determined to hold his ground. If he got in, maybe he could get her to talk, and if she did, he might find out what was wrong.

The irony of him, the loner who revealed nothing of his feelings, now wanting to find a way to get another human being, a woman no less, to reveal hers, rose to the surface. He grinned. Maybe it was Ezekiel, that frontier tell-it-like-it-is guy, who was still at work.

"I'm not really dressed for company," she began.

"You look fine to me." And she did. He added for good measure, "And proper, too, if you're worrying about that."

He didn't say proper for what, and he wasn't about to.

"It's just soup and grilled cheese."

"Great!" He smiled broadly. "I'm catered out."

"Well . . ." Reluctantly, she opened the door.

"Thanks." He walked inside her home, feeling like a knight of old who'd found the key to his lady's chastity belt. A major bridge had definitely been crossed.

Her house was small and neat, done in a country

style of wood and plaids, appropriate for the mountain area in which she lived. The walls were decorated in a mix of embroidered and needlepoint work, probably by her own hand. More human touches were evident in the newspapers on the sofa, a book open and turned face down on the coffee table, a glass half filled with what looked like iced tea on the side table. It was a far cry from the expensive and perfect Beverly Hills homes he'd been in, one of which he'd even contemplated buying for himself. And it was better. No wonder Redford and Russell built homes in Wyoming and Montana. This was so warm and comfortable. A small tortoiseshell cat appeared and rubbed against his legs, purring loudly.

"Meet Lolita," Pen said, smiling as she shut the door behind him. "She's named for obvious reasons."

"So I see." Richard leaned over and stroked the cat's head. The purring volume went up several notches, so he picked her up. The little cat snuggled into his arms, rubbing her face against his right bicep and immediately endearing herself to him.

Pen reached over and patted her cat, saying, "You're a sex kitten if there ever was one."

Her eyes went wide and she pulled her hand away, clearly annoyed with herself for mentioning sex, even in such an innocent way. Richard chose to ignore the remark, though he burned to follow up on it. So talk of sex might bother her. Maybe she didn't want him around because she was attracted to him.

Wishful thinking, he thought ... but he thought it anyway.

"I like your house," he said as they walked through the living/dining area to the kitchen.

She looked over her shoulder. "You're kidding."

"Why would I kid?"

She shrugged. "I don't know. You've been in Hollywood homes, and mine's just an everyman house."

"Or everywoman. You forget, I grew up in houses like this." "Houses" was the key word, he thought, remembering all the moves his family had made because of his father's engineering jobs. Not homes, not quite. Maybe he was lonely too long, like the song, and that was why he was getting domestically philosophical. His cure was within that sensuously flowing robe right in front of him. Whether a relationship with Pen would be short-term or long, only time would tell. In the meantime he'd admire the view. A few moments later he discovered one disadvantage to Pen's house. The walking distance to the kitchen was far too short.

Dinner was what Pen promised, although she dressed it up with a salad and fruit for dessert. She was awkward at first, and Richard found himself having to draw her out, a reverse from his usual manner. By the end of the meal, as they sat at the table dawdling over the last of dessert, she was relaxed with him again, the Pen he'd already come to know.

"I have miles of videotape," she told him, with a wry grin. "It's amazing what you can get in a week's time. And it's all a mishmash."

He chuckled. "I'm not surprised. You were having too much fun."

She was leaning forward slightly in her chair, and the cover-up gaped at the bodice, revealing a tantalizing glimpse of cleavage.

She sighed, the view momentarily even more enticing. "But what I needed to do was put all the camera crew on one tape, the electrical people on another, the scenery people together, the makeup people, the actors. That way I could have done a class period on special effects or acting or background. Instead, I've got Libby on with the best boy, and you followed by a stunt coordinator, each of you talking about something unrelated to the other. I wonder if that poor PR guy would shoot me if I did a complete retaping."

"He'd probably trash the set," Richard said.

Lolita put her front paws on his thigh, dangerously close to a sensitive area of his body, and began to knead her paws back and forth. Concern gave way when he realized she was blessedly declawed. His future children were safe from her. Stroking the cat on the shoulders, he continued, "Anyway, our PR guy ought to be happy. I agreed to do an interview for him."

"Which you hate," she said.

"Does it show?"

She nodded. "The look of disgust on your face was a dead giveaway. Why do you hate to do them?"

"It invades my privacy. They ask the same silly questions over and over again, or ask about things that have no bearing on the movie in question or filmmaking in general. Why can't I just do my work and go home?" He waved a hand, even though she never made a comment. "I know, I know. We have to create excitement, get people interested in the film, let them know it's going to be out there, when and what it's about, and even give them some tidbits that make them feel like insiders on the production."

"Boy, I could make a fortune with my videotapes, couldn't I?"

He chuckled. "Probably." Feeling that she'd warmed up to him, Richard got to his real mission. "Why have you been avoiding me on the set?"

"I have?"

"Pen." He shook his head. "You're going to have to give a better performance of innocence than that. I'm an actor, and I learned my craft in England at Gielgud's knee."

He had gone to England with the idea of training as a Shakespearian actor. But coming under the eye of Sir John was what put him on this road.

"Did anybody ever tell you name-dropping is bad form?" she asked, making a face at him.

"Yes, but I never pay attention to it. Did I offend

you in some way last week? If I have, I'm sorry. I didn't mean to."

"No," she said, looking stricken. "I'm sorry, Richard, that you even had that impression."

"Then what is the problem?"

She looked everywhere but at his face.

"Pen."

"Okay." She fiddled with her paper napkin a few seconds longer, than took a deep breath. "I've ... I've become a fan. There's obviously no future in becoming a Richard Creighton hanger-on. You'll be gone in a few weeks, a couple of months at most, and I'll still be here." She shrugged. "So it seemed best to me that I start now to avoid a mistake in the making."

The blood buzzed in his ears at the thought of her as a screaming fan who wanted to throw herself at him. Not Pen. She was too sane and sensible. He already knew that. But what she had done was to tell him any relationship between them was out of the question because it would be of short duration—exactly the type of relationship he didn't want to have with her. She had touched something in him that he wanted to explore thoroughly before he could let it go.

"I'm sorry," he said. "But I can't accept that."

Her eyes widened and her jaw dropped. She straightened up in her chair. "What do you mean, you can't accept that?"

He didn't know what to say to not have the conversation blow up in his face. How Cary Grant would handle it came to mind, so he spelled, "I c-a-n-t a-c-c-e-p-t t-h-a-t."

"I can spell."

"So what part of it didn't you get?" he asked, grinning.

"If you were eight, I'd have sent you to the principal's office for that," she said, eyeing him sternly.

"Good thing I'm thirty-four." He was liking this verbal flirting. "Does this mean I get a spanking instead? Please say yes."

"I'm not kinky that way."

"Then what way are you kinky?"

"Very funny, but I saw 'Moonlighting.' " Pen stood up and gathered the plates. "You're no Bruce Willis, Richard. I think I'll do the dishes."

Richard chuckled. He knew a surrender flag going up when he saw it.

Pen and Richard sat on her tiny back patio, screened from prying eyes by a rose trellis. She should have gotten rid of him directly after dinner, but he'd suggested one more iced tea. *One.* And she had thought it better to be nice than bitchy, for Libby's sake. Sure. Honesty made her admit she loved his company. But she had told him enough of how he made her feel without revealing even more of her emotional vulnerability.

She was determined to steer clear of dangerous waters, but couldn't entirely stem her curiosity about him.

"So what was it like, studying in England?" she asked.

"It was terrific," he replied. "Good for an actor. Have you been there?"

"Yes, for a ten-day vacation." She smiled, remembering. "I loved it, although I felt as if I'd gone back to the sixties. I don't know what reminded me of that."

"It's a slower and more innocent lifestyle." He grinned. "You should go from there directly to Los Angeles. You feel you've stepped onto another planet."

"I'll bet."

She could feel awareness stirring her blood. From the moment she'd opened her front door to discover him on her threshold, she had felt shaky. Her desire for him had been growing steadily since. She couldn't look at his face without studying the lines that were arrestingly sharp now and would be handsomely craggy in twenty years. She couldn't look at his upper body without noting the wide shoulders. She couldn't look at his arms without wanting to touch the well-defined muscles and the dusting of dark hairs. And she couldn't look at his hands without wondering what they'd do to her body with their touch.

He reached over and took her hand. Pen froze even as his strong, warm fingers entwined with her own. The heat of him gave her a momentary jolt. She took a deep breath to counteract the sensation. If he was aware of her hesitation, he never showed it. He just held her hand.

"I don't tell people very much about myself," he said, shrugging. "It wasn't easy going from town to town every few years. You gain a friend or two and then you have to leave them." He turned away. "Sort of like this. But we all need friends."

Next he'd be asking her to be his neighbor, Pen thought. Mister Rogers had nothing on this guy for making a person aware of her shortcomings. How could she ignore this appeal to be friends?

She couldn't. The moment he'd said it, she knew she couldn't. But she didn't have to be more than friends.

"Of course we all need friends," she said smoothly, patting his hand. "And that's what I want to be, Richard. A friend. Not a . . . fan."

He turned back to her and frowned, as if he didn't like the words. Pen smiled brightly at him and squeezed his hand in assurance. Friendly assurance.

In return, Richard leaned across the two arms of the chairs and kissed her.

His mouth was hungry yet gentle, and any thought of resistance went right out of Pen's head. If this was friendship, then she wanted more. She gripped his arms to anchor herself, marveling at the feel of the long, ropy muscles beneath her fingers. He was all lean strength, just enough. Just right.

Her senses had been spinning long before the kiss deepened. Richard's fingers threaded through her hair, the pressure soft yet demanding, his palm cupping her chin. The touch was almost too much to bear, and her blood turned thick and hot in her veins, pulsing deeply through her system. The kiss went on and on until she was moaning in the back of her throat and practically clinging to him. His hand curved around her breast, his palm pressed across her nipple.

Need rocked through her, and she couldn't stand it any longer. She pressed herself to him, his chest a solid wall that satisfied her and left her yearning for more at the same time. Both his hands found her breasts, the caresses going on and on, driving her higher and higher. She had wanted this so much and yet thought she would scream with frustration because she wanted so much more. His fingers continually grazed the hardened points of her nipples, while her fingers fluttered over his shoulders, clenching and unclenching.

Suddenly he pulled himself away and shot out of the chair. "I . . . I have to go now."

"Wha . . . ?" Pen blinked at him in bewilderment, her head spinning.

"I have to go." He looked everywhere but at her. "Thanks for dinner."

She realized her arms were still curved in an empty embrace and dropped them into her lap, mortified at the telltale giveaway and confused over what had happened. "Richard—"

"I have to go before . . . we need to be sure about this." He disappeared back into her house without waiting for her to escort him. Before she could gather her wits and move, she heard her front door open and close.

Pen felt deflated. Richard had said they needed to be sure about this. But all she knew for sure was that one moment they were kissing and in the next he was disappearing faster than an ice block in a sauna.

She leaned her head back in the chair and put her hands over her face.

She'd think about this tomorrow.

He had been a perfect gentleman, Richard thought as he climbed into his trailer that night. Absolutely perfect, and it had almost killed him.

He wanted Pen, wanted her very badly. But he needed her to feel the same way. And he didn't want to rush things. He wished he was more prepared to handle this, but he'd been alone too long. Nuances of relationships always seemed to escape him. But tonight he was on the right track. He had to be.

So why did he need a cold shower? And why did he think there were a lot of them in his future?

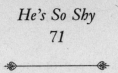

"Pen, we've got a problem," Libby began the next morning.

Not compared to hers, Pen thought as Richard emerged from his dressing trailer and crossed the set, distracting her from her cousin's monologue. They were at a new location, up on cliffs above a quarry lake, about ten miles from Blairstown, although filming had been delayed for some reason this morning. But the rugged backdrop only emphasized Richard's brooding looks—especially since she'd had tons of time to observe him. He, the real Richard, fit here in this lonely place.

Oh, boy, but she had the groupie fever bad. She never should have invited him into her home, let alone kissed him. More than a kiss, she reminded herself. It had been like falling off one of these cliffs. If he hadn't stopped things . . . at least that's what she concluded he'd been doing. Despite continual self-reminders that this would be no more than a fling for him, a reckless, live-for-the-moment part of her wanted him—and damn the emotional consequences he'd leave behind.

" . . . so you'll do it. Thanks a bunch. You're terrific. I told them you'd be happy to help out. Makeup! Wardrobe!" Libby shouted out.

"What makeup? What wardrobe? What help out?" Pen babbled, staring at her cousin.

Libby turned to her in exasperation as people came running from all directions. "The actress who was supposed to do the scene is sick, and the idiot girl never said a word to anyone! We've set all this up for the rescue scene, you know the one I mean, and not a word from that girl! How the hell am I supposed to stay on schedule for the studio when some ditzy actress, the only one for the scene, doesn't even show up for work? And she'll get paid for it, dammit! The actors' union'll see to that."

"But, but," Pen sputtered as the horrible realization set in that Libby meant for *her* to take the missing actress's place. "There has to be another actress around, Libby! I can't do it!"

"Of course you can. It's simple. You go over the cliff with Richard to save yourselves from the Indians. All you've got to do is fall, for goodness sake! And there isn't another actress around. We don't have extra people on the set unless we need them, because we have to pay them. Union rules. By the way, you'll have to join the union. See Jerry, who'll arrange for that today. It's irregular, but it's happened before."

"But, but—"

The makeup and wardrobe masters swarmed around her, cutting off her words. Libby said, "Okay, people, you've got a half hour to get her into shape. You'll be great, Pen. Absolutely great. I'll make sure you get in the credits. See? A little nepotism goes a long way. And just think of the great physics lesson you can teach on this: Can a woman fall faster than a man?"

"No, she can't!" Pen wailed as she was hauled away by people discussing her size, shape, and color over her head.

Thirty minutes later, right on the dot, she found herself transformed into a colonial settler with striped skirt, white low-cut blouse cinched by a woman's brown weskit, and heavy black buckled shoes, all appropriately dirtied. A dingy mobcap had been pulled over her forehead, her hair completely hidden, and half her face obscured by the wide ruffle around the cap.

In wardrobe, Pen realized that the fall couldn't be really dangerous. They'd never risk actors—and especially not the star—if it were. They'd get a stuntman and stuntwoman for this scene if the action posed any threat.

She had to admit that the prospect of being in a movie was exciting. She'd be the envy of everyone in the teachers' room at school.

"You look great!" Libby said. "Richard! Come see your costar for today."

Richard walked over to them. Pen braced herself, feeling the tremor in her smile at finally facing him after last night. They had seemed to avoid actually speaking to each other all morning. He halted when he caught sight of her face under the cap.

"You can't be serious, Libby," he said, eyeing Pen up and down. "Pen's no actress."

Pen bristled. "I don't actually have to act, only fall off a cliff."

He glared at her. "I know you have to fall off the cliff. Have you even looked at the drop? It's no piece of cake. This is work for stunt people."

"Oh, bull," Libby broke in.

"They wouldn't risk *you* if they thought you'd get hurt," Pen said, stiffening her spine.

Richard just snorted in disgust, giving Pen the distinct impression that he knew exactly what Libby and the studio would risk. "Do you think this is your big break? Is that why you're doing this?"

Pen clenched her jaw to control her temper, then spat out, "I've jumped off high places before. I'm not scared."

"Only idiotic!"

"It's okay," Libby said, hastily intervening. "Anyway, we can't hold up the filming. And Pen volunteered."

Pen shot her cousin a look, ready to open her mouth again. Instead, she clamped her jaw shut. This was some greeting from the man who had kissed her senseless the night before.

Richard turned and strode away, his body stiff with anger.

"See?" Libby said, turning to follow him. "Everything'll be fine."

Pen brought up the rear, cursing under her breath all the way. Richard's moods changed like night and day. She'd never understand him. And what was that last crack about a big break? The only thing she'd be breaking was her neck.

A look over the cliff showed a two-story drop into a lake. Pen swallowed. It was about as high as an Olympic platform diving board, she estimated. But the big question was, how deep was the lake?

"How deep is the lake?" she asked, deciding not to pass on the question of the year.

"Not deep enough to make this jump a piece of cake," Richard muttered, walking away after his own look.

"It's fine," Libby said, waving at the stunt coordinator. "Bob'll tell you. Won't you, Bob?"

Bob made an unreadable gesture. "Jump out, not down, and you should be okay."

Pen glanced down and swallowed. *Out, not down. Out, not down. Broken neck, not dead. Get out of this now.* Breathing deeply, she said, "You're only in the movies once. I'm ready."

Libby whisked her away, positioning her on the mark. Several Indians positioned themselves about twenty yards from her, the grins on their faces the only accessories to their loincloths. Hell, she thought, was Libby filming an accurately costumed movie or a Chippendale dancers reunion?

Richard took a stance close to her. Her breath suddenly went shallow, and her chest still felt tight.

He muttered, "I can't believe you're doing this."

"What was I supposed to do? Have your precious filming for the day go down the drain? Have Libby murder me for saying no?" Her hands were shaking. She wasn't sure whether her reaction was from anger, excitement, arousal, or healthy fear.

He took her arm. "Yes, that's exactly what you're suppose to do. Dammit, Pen, you don't know what you're doing. You'll get hurt—"

"It's an opportunity," she interrupted, his touch distracting. "The kids—"

"You're not some damn experiment!"

"Okay!" Libby shouted, interrupting the argument. "Richard, you and the settler woman have been caught outside the fort by the Chickasaw scouting party. This woman has been coming on to you . . . you're in love with Robertson's wife, Charlotte . . . but there's no hope there and so you intended to temporarily lose your pain with this woman . . ."

Pen realized she was playing the fort's whore. Great, she thought. The school board would probably fire her the instant the film came out.

" . . . but you let your guard down and are now responsible for placing her in danger," Libby continued, giving the motivation for the scene. "You have *got* to save her, or you won't be able to live with yourself. You have burst out of the woods from your interrupted interlude, which is already on schedule to film tomorrow, by the way, so I'm *sure* Julie will be better for that." Libby glanced slowly around at the crew, imparting the clear message that somebody had better tell this to the missing Julie. "Pen, when I say 'Action,' you just run like hell and follow Richard's lead. *Don't* anticipate the jump! Richard leads the girl right up over the edge of the 'bluffs' of the 'Cumberland River.' That's the quarry lake here. Oh, and scream while you're going down."

Pen nodded, not trusting her voice. *Run like hell, follow Richard's lead. Jump out, not down, but look like you don't know to jump out, not down. And remember to scream.* She had a feeling the last instruction was going to be a cinch to follow.

"Pen, please," Richard said, his voice low. "Tell Libby you can't do this."

Pen stared at him. He cared about her, really cared about her. "I—"

"Action!" Libby yelled.

"Run, woman! Run if you value your life!" Richard bellowed into her face, his whole being transforming in an instant into Ezekiel Freemont.

He grabbed her hand, yanking her off her feet, and broke into a dead run. She stumbled over the long skirts and nearly fell before she could grab them up out of the way with her left hand. Richard dragged her along, never stopping for her. The men behind her whooped loudly, clearly seeing the chance she was inadvertently giving them to catch up, the sound so close it raised the hairs on the back of her neck. They'd be overtaken, she thought, and Libby would kill her. Pen put on a burst of speed, the awkward shoes in danger of slipping on the smooth dirt and stones, until she was not only keeping up with Richard but almost passing him.

They ran neck and neck in a sprint that Secretariat would have been proud of. A second later the ground dropped off under their feet, and Pen found herself sailing through the air.

"Woooeeee!" Richard yelled joyously.

The skirts flew up over her face, blocking her view, and she screamed in panic at not being able to see. She frantically pushed them down with her free hand and then she was plunging into ice-cold water. It hit her with a smack, taking her breath. The skirts came over her head and shoulders again, this time entrapping her in their smothering arms as the water closed over her head and took her down into its depths. She pushed the skirts out of way again, but could feel them pulling heavily at her legs when she tried to swim up to the surface. Richard's hand was on her arm still, dragging her up with him as he swam. Her lungs began to clamor for air, telling her that despite her efforts she was far too slow. She kicked and pushed ever upward in yet another race, this one truly dangerous if she lost.

She broke the surface with a whoosh. The water sucked her back in over her head, but she forced her way up, treading to keep her head above the surface. Richard was next to her, and she could feel the water swirling around both of them, like a sensual bond entrapping them together. His hair was plastered to his head, and water streamed off his face, beading his lashes.

"You okay?" he asked.

She grinned, even though the skirts and shoes were heavy. Pushing the drooping mobcap out of her eyes, she pronounced, "I'm great!"

He grinned back, nudging her with him as he swam closer to the shore. When their feet touched bottom, he stopped her and started to chuckle. "I ought to shoot you for doing this. You make me crazy."

"Do I?"

"You do."

"You left last night so abruptly."

Those gorgeous eyes widened. "For you. I don't want to rush you."

"You didn't talk to me this morning."

"I was afraid I'd do what Ezekiel intended with the fort woman. If I had known it would be you . . . I like you, Pen."

She swallowed. "You do?"

He pulled her to him, into the circle of his arms. Into his warmth. "I do."

He kissed her. His mouth was wet, his lips cool . . . but his tongue was warm, warming her. She ran her hands through his hair, delighting in the feel of the wet strands and the heat of his skin. Her skirts wrapped around both their legs, unsteadying them for an instant and breaking off the kiss.

"Very nice!" Libby called out above them. "But you're suppose to be drowned now, Pen, not kissing our guilt-ridden man here."

They looked up to see not only Libby but everyone else crowded along the edge of the cliff. Pen blushed, horrified to realize that the entire crew had seen the kiss.

"Okay," Libby called out, breaking up the audience. "Pull 'em out, blow dry 'em off and into makeup again. I want to get a second take in the can."

"I can't!" Pen exclaimed, in shock. Once over the cliff into madness was quite enough.

"Too late," Richard said, grinning.

As she looked into those green-green eyes that mirrored the humor and intelligence within the man, she knew it was too late for a lot of things. Even as her heart lifted up, she knew she was sunk.

Richard took her hand and pulled her to shore.

FIVE

"Are you free for an after-dinner walk?" Richard asked the moment Pen opened her front door.

He couldn't help smiling to himself as she stared at him in bewilderment. She was in that flowing caftan again, the seeming de rigueur fashion for her evenings. Didn't she get out? He wasn't complaining, he decided, only wondering.

"An after-dinner walk?" she repeated, blinking.

"It's after dinner," Richard reminded her. In fact, the last rays of the summer sun were tilting over the mountains, turning the sky a muted orange-gray. "I thought we'd go along the pond behind the waterworks building and take the footbridge on the academy side." His gaze lowered to the curves of her breasts. The thin silky material beautifully draped their fullness. Blood began to pulse in his veins, lightly, controllable still—but not if he continued to stare . . . and imagine.

He shifted his gaze to her face, and found himself mesmerized by the slight tangling of her hair. The strands seemed to curl in and around each other as if his fingers had threaded their way through them. He leaned slightly forward. "A walk in the moonlight, Pen. It can be very romantic."

"I'm never sure who you are at any given moment," she said wistfully.

He chuckled. "Me neither, sometimes. Can I just be Richard tonight?"

She sighed. "I shouldn't. But I've been doing a lot of things I shouldn't lately. Like jumping off cliffs. Come on in while I get changed."

She opened the door wider, and he stepped inside. Lolita immediately rushed to greet him, meowing her pleasure at his arrival and rubbing against his legs.

"She certainly knows how to welcome people," Richard said, picking up the cat and placing her in the crook of his arm. He petted her, and she purred loudly.

"Good thing she's not a watchdog," Pen said. "I'd be lucky if the house was still standing."

She excused herself, and Richard watched her go upstairs, belatedly realizing how stiff the undercurrents had been for two people who had kissed passionately in front of a crowd just hours earlier. Maybe she was tired from the strain of the two jumps. After all, this was different for her, hardly the usual school day.

He went to the foot of the stairs. "Are you okay after today's jumps?" he shouted up to her.

"Fine!" she called back, her voice muffled through a closed door. Now she sounded strong, not particularly tired. Richard shrugged.

A walk, he told himself firmly. He might be feeling like jumping from the rooftops, but he should try to keep his euphoria under control, he warned himself. Still, he felt on top of the world—and all because of that very public kiss he and Pen had shared. With it he'd declared himself for all to see, and for some reason that open commitment made him feel ecstatic.

Pen came back downstairs a few minutes later, dressed in beige walking shorts and a blue and white shirt, the sleeves rolled up above her elbows. Her hair was pulled back in a ponytail and held by a blue ribbon. Richard thought she looked gorgeous.

"We'll probably get eaten alive by the mosquitoes," she commented.

"No, we won't," he said, putting Lolita on the floor and shooing her into the living room with a gentle pat on the rump.

Pen laughed as they went out the front door. "You've been away from New Jersey too long."

"I have a special survival technique for keeping the mosquitoes away," he said, standing on her doorstep.

"Really? What's that?"

He pulled a small aerosol can out of his back pocket. "Bug spray."

Pen burst into laughter. "Stinker!"

"That's what we'll be after this. Here, hold out your arm."

She did, while saying, "You know everyone thinks you're using bear grease or some other old-fashioned survival trick, making yourself another Daniel Boone."

"Daniel Boone would have killed for some of this stuff. Besides, I've got to be me once in a while, and this is definitely one of those times." He took her by the wrist and sprayed a light dose of the repellent along her arm. Her skin was warm to his touch, and silken. His hand enclosed her wrist easily, the feminine bone and muscle seemingly fragile yet having a resilient strength.

He got them both sprayed with a minimum of fuss, and they began their walk toward the old waterworks building, now the town library. The pond and the footbridge lay behind it.

"Too bad we didn't have anyone videotaping your performance today for your class," he said, casually taking her hand in his. He felt like a kid on his first date, all nervous and making calculated moves. He'd never acquired the knack for the body language involved in a man-woman relationship, the years of shyness having blinded him to the adolescent lessons on the subject. If it was required of a character, he had no hesitation. Real life was another matter altogether.

To his relief, she didn't pull her hand away. "Actually, Libby promised to put the jump on video-tape for the kids. She said she'd spring for something called a film-to-tape transfer. Does that sound right?"

Richard nodded.

"Gee, I'm so thrilled."

He chuckled. "You'll have your very own video of a classic moment."

The streets of Blairstown, even on a fine summer's night, had little traffic; the town was always dead with the summer vacation at the academy. Richard had heard the grumbles of complaint about the lack of amusement for a cast and crew used to the twenty-four-hour day, sophisticated fast-paced life in Los Angeles or New York. No wonder Libby was pushing the filming, to keep them all from exploding with boredom.

But he liked it, this little stretch of small towns, large farms, and steep, wooded mountainsides. The pace was leisurely, not frenetic. He felt he could make his own mark here, without pretense—no acting, no hiding behind characters, nothing but being his own true self. Pen had made it, that was obvious. She was comfortable with herself and her life. He envied her.

The old waterworks building loomed ahead, its architecture faux-medieval. They ducked underneath an arch, then turned along the path running parallel to the side of the building.

The sky had deepened to a blue that matched Pen's shirt; the rush of water spilling over the man-made fall was almost musical; the iron and wooden footbridge directly above at the neck of the pond looked like a miniature train bridge in the lower light of sunset. White bubbles churned in the foam as the water was swept along into the culvert under the town. The gentle roar of it overlaid all other sounds. The first star twinkled overhead.

Richard escorted Pen up a cement path to the stone steps that climbed back up the hillside on the left side of the stream. The first buildings of Blair Academy rose at the crest of the hill. The high walls along the steps built sixty years before enclosed them as they made their way.

"Every time I walk here, I expect Dracula to appear suddenly on the landing up there," Pen said, smiling. "Or Barnabas Collins from 'Dark Shadows,' the Ben Cross version."

"It's got all the elements of a gothic," Richard replied, smiling wryly at her choice of vampires. She *would* pick Ben. He had tested for *Chariots of Fire* when he'd been in England and lost out to the man. He continued, "Ominous buildings on the hill . . . shortcuts along the pond . . . nice dark night to cover the series of murders."

"You make it sound like *Friday the Thirteenth, Part Forty-Seven.*"

"Is that what they're up to now? I didn't know."

"Hmm, must be. Too bad the girls from the college are all at home. Or you wouldn't be walking this path. You'd be running for your life."

"I wouldn't mind being a sex symbol," he said, thinking of his teenage years when he'd been skinny and gawky and withdrawn.

"Be careful what you wish for," Pen reminded him. "Or you just might get it. Ask Fabio."

"Who?"

"Never mind."

He stopped her on the first landing, the one she envisioned as Barnabas's staging platform. "Pen."

"What?" Awareness came into her eyes even as she murmured the word.

Richard drew her to him. He kissed her, gently at first, then with more fervor as the softness of her lips sent his head spinning. Her tongue played with his, in a prelude to a more intimate dance between man and woman. Her shirt was no barrier to the feel of her body, her nipples already hard against his chest. Her skin was warm on his palms, heating his own flesh even more, and her fingers gripped his shoulders, clenching and unclenching. Her perfume overwhelmed his senses. He knew the scent of her would stay with him forever.

He finally raised his head, but only to return again for another devastating kiss. He curved his hand around her breast, feeling the hardness of her nipple along the pad of his thumb. She moaned in the back of her throat at his touch.

"Ahhh . . . I shouldn't," she whispered, her arms wrapped tightly around his shoulders. "But I can't help myself with you."

He raised his head. "You have no idea how that makes me feel."

She pressed her hips to his. "Oh yes I do."

His physical reaction to her might be all-encompassing, but that was only a part of what she made him feel. Invincible was the other. Emotionally invincible.

He brought his mouth down to hers again, the kiss going wild now.

Voices from above them, faint but drawing closer, finally caught his attention. Richard reluctantly let Pen go. Her hair was half out of her ponytail, and her shirt was rumpled. He had a feeling his looked no better.

"You're a mess," they both whispered at the same time, then laughed softly together.

Richard raked his fingers through his hair to tame it while Pen tucked in her shirt. She was still fiddling with the ribbon in her hair as they began to climb the steps again. Above them, several people walked into view. Richard recognized them as members of the crew.

Everyone said hello and passed by each other, a couple of the men grinning at Richard in the process. He shook his head. Crews that worked well together were like family, a bunch of brothers and sisters; there was always a lot of teasing and playfulness in such a crew. He'd just have to live with the ribbing he was bound to get, he decided, watching the sway of Pen's derriere as he mounted the steps behind her. He certainly wasn't about to give her up.

The end of filming and his going away were becoming more and more repugnant to him. Yet it was far too soon to think seriously of other things . . . wasn't it?

He was pondering the question when they came to the top of the stairs. Pen led them out to the middle of the bridge and they turned to watch the pond, its water oddly still as the water in the man-made stream behind them continually rushed. Ducks were dark shapes on the surface of the water. Old Victorian homes, their lights winking, dotted the steep banks of the pond, which was in their backyards. Higher up on their left was the academy.

"Beautiful," Richard murmured, gazing at Pen's profile as she leaned against the narrow iron railing of the bridge.

She turned her head slightly and smiled at him.

What was he going to do?

Pen walked hand in hand with Richard. She was surrendering with every step of the walk home. Hell, she thought, it hadn't even been a decent fight in the first place. She'd wanted him, right from the beginning, moodiness or not. And in moments like these, when the veneer slipped aside to reveal the quiet, shy man underneath, she was an absolute goner. If he had been slicker, more sophisticated, her resolve would have been intact, because she would have known that sex was all there was to his interest. But she knew a deeper relationship was possible with Richard. Very possible. And completely doomed. They were from two entirely different worlds now, each alien to the other. How could they overcome that? She pushed the thought aside, hating it.

They meandered through the streets of Blairstown, just enjoying the evening and each other's company, lingering along as if neither wanted the walk to end. But in the back of Pen's mind was that ending and how she would not be able to resist inviting him into her house. And into her bed. Need had come that far that fast for her.

When they reached her house, he kissed her at her door, under her porch light. Sensations wrapped around her, insulating her in their drugging warmth.

When he finally lifted his head, his breath was harsh to her ears, as if he couldn't get enough air into his lungs. She had made him that way, she thought in triumph at her feminine power.

"Richard, come inside," she murmured, kissing him lightly.

His arms tightened around her. He buried his face in her hair. "I . . . I can't."

She blinked. He let her go, all but her hand. He held it tightly, as if it were a lifeline.

"I want to," he said. "You don't know how much I want to. But we're not kids, Pen. I want more than sex with you. I want it right. I can wait until you're sure."

"Richard, I . . ." But she couldn't say what she was sure about because she wasn't sure about anything.

He smiled. "I can wait."

He left her with a last kiss that had her melting into the step. She stared after him until he crested the top of the hill and disappeared over the other side.

"Dammit," she muttered, even as she sighed.

She'd finally found an honorable man.

"Okay, today's scene is the semi-love scene, kissus interruptus, if you will," Libby said, chuckling at her own joke.

Richard kept the impatience he felt from showing on his face. The set was an open one, the scene today fairly innocent. That still didn't make the intimacy required easy to maintain in front of others. In front of Pen. He was wishing that she, not Julie, waited to do the love scene with him. Instead, he had Julie, looking stricken from Libby's earlier chastising for not showing up for the jump. The whole mix made Richard anticipate a long, uncomfortable day.

He concentrated on Ezekiel's emotional frustration as Libby went over the blocking for the scene. But his concentration failed him often, and his gaze kept shifting to Pen. He surveyed the creamy skin at her throat, the smile playing along her full lower lip, the guileless expression in her vivid blue eyes. How, he wondered in disgust, could he have left her last night? That damned Ezekiel must have surfaced with all his frontier chivalry. She'd asked him inside, into her bed. There was no mistaking the invitation. She'd *asked* him.

And he'd refused out of a sense of nobility. He wanted more with her, but he'd wind up with nothing if he wasn't careful. Next invitation—

"Got it?"

Richard glanced sharply at Libby, who was peering back at him skeptically. Julie looked half determined and half scared, obviously knowing this was a big break for a young actress to play a scene with the lead. And the lead had only been listening with half an ear to the director. The commercial was right, he thought. *Never let them see you sweat.* He said, "Got it."

Libby's smile was more of a knowing leer. "Good. Positions, then. Ready on the set!"

Everyone immediately took up his place. Richard closed his mind to everything except the scene and his character. Libby shouted, "Action!" and they did their bit of dialogue. Then he grabbed Julie's hand and strode forward at a fast clip toward the woods ahead, taking her away from the other "settlers." They were supposed to move under the shelter of the trees, then begin to "make love" against the trunk of a large and very old oak. Julie giggled on cue behind him, amused at Ezekiel's haste as he pulled her along. She provided just the right amount of resistance to make her seem coquettish, yet the woman of easy virtue she was playing.

Richard brought them both to the first tree and turned to Julie. She tilted her head up, her expression all wanton invitation. Richard inclined his head in a way he knew would give the camera a good angle of the kiss, but hide the acting, then put his lips to hers and wiggled his head from side to side in a fair imitation of passion. The mock kiss went on for about a minute, with either he or his partner moving their hands around each other's back and shoulders. Richard sensed Julie was as conscious and as careful of camera position as he. He refused even to think about Pen, knowing the acted kiss might very well turn real for him if he did. He wanted only real kisses with the real thing, not a substitute.

"Cut!"

Richard parted immediately from Julie—and he didn't look at Pen, knowing he had to keep himself focused as an actor.

"Okay, that was great," Libby said, coming toward them. "Now on to the second kiss. I want you, Richard, to sweep your hand down her back, like this." Libby took his hand and illustrated on Julie's back. "Julie, your hand goes to Richard's hair, thread your fingers through it, then move your hand to his shirt and begin fiddling with the opening. You're more the aggressor here. Richard, you put her back against the tree trunk and rub your body against hers. Make it more desperate than passionate, because you are trying to get rid of your feelings for Charlotte through this woman."

Libby called for action, and they followed her direction to a tee. Richard put desperation into his movements. A corner of his mind was amused as always in these scenes, knowing how realistic they looked on screen and exactly how each gesture was choreographed through a series of cuts and takes.

Libby called cut again when she was satisfied.

"Okay," she went on. "on this next kiss, Richard, your hands go to her bodice to unlace it, and that's when you hear the noise. A faint snap, unnatural in the forest. You freeze. Your head comes up. You belatedly sense the danger. You grab the girl and run. Julie, you resist, keep asking what's wrong. Richard, you don't answer, you don't have time, just keeping yanking her along. Got it?"

Richard nodded.

Libby called for action again, and the scene followed its course, right to the point where Pen's jump meshed with it. Richard sighed with relief when it was over.

"Thanks," Julie said, smiling in gratitude.

"You did a good job," he told her.

As filming halted, Richard ducked around to Pen.

"I'm glad that's done," he said, grinning at her. "Love scenes are grueling."

Pen admitted silently that she felt the same. But it hadn't been as bad as she'd feared. At first, when she realized it would be a love scene, she'd wanted both to protest and run away at the same time. But with the constant cuts by Libby, she realized how directed everything was . . . how clinical. Viewed without benefit of camera lens angles, the kiss wasn't even that. Just kind of a "let's look like we're really kissing passionately when we're not." Acting, she thought. Every love scene in any movie she would see in the future would be a big disappointment now that she knew how it was created.

"It wasn't what I expected," she said finally.

He chuckled. "Thank God. Actors find them the hardest to do, to look intimate when one isn't."

"As long as one isn't," Pen said, then flushed.

But Richard's grin only widened. He looked downright happy with that jealous-sounding announcement. Okay, she thought, so she was jealous. But she did have a demonstration today of how little a woman needed to fear from this sort of thing. On the other hand, clinical though it might be, it wasn't great to watch.

"There you are!"

Pen turned with Richard at the sound of the voice. A woman waved at them as she strode their way. She was dressed in an oversize white blouse tied at the waist, her unbound nipples dark under the thin material. Her outrageously tight jeans delineated the cleft at the junction of her thighs. Despite the sunglasses she wore, she was instantly recognizable as Mary Jane Stevens, Richard's costar.

With her wide smile, she looked friendly enough, Pen thought, remembering the suddenly closed expressions when her name had come up at Libby's makeshift dinner party. A moment later Pen discovered just how friendly Mary Jane could be.

"Nobody kisses my man but me," Mary Jane said, and plastered her mouth against Richard's.

SIX

Richard knew immediately that Mary Jane was attempting to throw him off balance and gain control of the political food chain on the set. Actors did it in different ways. They could be difficult to work with, or they could skip etiquette and go right to the producer with complaints. Or they could put their costars at some kind of an emotional disadvantage.

Mary Jane actually tried to wrap her leg around his thigh. Having had more than enough of the little game, Richard gently pushed her away.

"Nice to meet you, too, Mary Jane," he said, matter-of-factly, refusing to give her an inch on the control scale. "I'm looking forward to working with you. This is Pen Marsh, Libby's cousin and a friend of mine, who's visiting the set."

"Hello," Mary Jane said coolly, barely turning her head in Pen's direction.

"How lovely to meet you," Pen replied, just as coolly.

Libby called Mary Jane away before she could do something even more outrageous.

"Trouble has arrived," Richard muttered, leaning against his rifle and watching Mary Jane go.

"Really?"

He glanced at Pen, who raised dubious eyebrows. He grinned and took her arm. She *was* jealous, he thought happily. Her earlier remark had seemed to indicate her proprietary feelings for him, although he'd wondered if his interpretation had been overenthusiastic. Now he knew. Escorting her away from the set, he said, "You certainly know how to make a man feel good."

"I do?"

"You do. Let's take a walk."

"I think we're already doing that."

"Good, then I'm on the right track." He sighed. "I wish actors weren't so damned insecure."

"It seems to go with the territory."

"The stunt Mary Jane just pulled was to fluster me and show right from the first that she is really the dominant actor on the set."

"Don't hyenas do that sort of thing?"

"Very funny." They were under the shade of the trees on the edge of the meadow, far enough away to be out of earshot yet close enough for Richard to see when he was wanted again. He settled his back against a tree trunk and slid down to comfortably hunker at its base. Pen found a large, fairly flat rock and sat on it.

"Are you upset about that love scene?" he asked.

She looked away, then back. "I don't have a right to be."

"What if I give you the right?" His chest tightened with the question, more painful for him to ask than she'd probably ever know. If he felt invincible before, he felt very vulnerable now.

"If you gave me the right, would you still do them?"

The answer was as automatic as breathing. "If they were essential to the story line, yes."

"And if they weren't, you would object for your own integrity, not out of concern for anyone else's feelings." She smiled slightly. "You've asked a question that has no meaning, Richard."

"Yes, it does," he countered stubbornly. "It matters personally."

"And how can I, even if given the right, ask someone I care about to compromise themselves for my sake? Either you accept what someone needs to do or you don't."

The heart of the matter was a lot more than a movie's love scene, and he believed that she knew it. "Do you care about me?"

She was silent for so long that his heart began to pound with anxiety. Finally she said, "I told you before, I have a crush on you. You're exciting, Richard. You dazzle. Your attentions flatter. And yet there's something more. I feel vulnerable, and I don't like it."

"So am I, Pen." He drew in a breath to steady himself.

Pen rose to her feet. "I don't think I'm coming to the set anymore, Richard."

"What!" He stood up, his whole body tense.

"I . . ." She shrugged. "I don't have anything more I can do with my school project unless I retape the whole thing, so I'm back to being a nuisance."

"Pen, don't let Mary Jane throw you," he began.

"It isn't Mary Jane. Well, yes, in a way it is. She reminded me I have no place here and how easily I can get in people's way." She grinned. "Besides, once you jump off a cliff, the thrill is gone."

"What about me?" he asked, feeling oddly helpless. She was slipping away, and he didn't know how to stop her. "I like having you here to talk to, to be around." He was making her sound like a hanger-on, exactly what she was so afraid she was. "You've become a part of the set. I know everyone likes you. You've shown us all how to tolerate Libby, for one thing. And you keep her from turning into a little Hitler, for another."

"Glad I served a purpose." She shook her head.

"No, Richard. I think I'm better off doing this. I think you are too."

She walked away from him, heading back to where the cars were parked.

Richard felt totally bereft. In one fell swoop, he had lost her companionship, as well as the invitation to her bed. How the hell it had happened, he had no idea.

And he had no idea about how to get it all back.

"You know, Lolita, there are actually times when I envy you," Pen said to her cat, who was stretched out on her chest, purring away to beat the band. "So, are you seeing Buster next door tonight?"

Lolita's purrs went up a notch at the neighboring cat's name, but she didn't move from her contented perch. Pen stroked the cat's soft fur. She really did wish she had Lolita's ability to accept whatever was offered with no regrets if it didn't last. But she couldn't.

Okay, so she had run from Mary Jane. Anyone would, rather than subject themselves to what would be a continual battle of comeuppance. She had a feeling Mary Jane already knew about Richard and her—what little there was to know—and would use it against him. Them. Pen thought of simply refusing to play the star's game, but Mary Jane would probably be undeterred. Someone who so obviously needed to manipulate wouldn't be able to quit for lack of players.

She'd suck them into her games again. No wonder dead silence had accompanied the mere mention of her name at Libby's.

Worse, even if Richard wasn't interested in Mary Jane, who could compete with her? That body, that overt sensuality . . . Pen shuddered. She didn't even want to compete with Mary Jane.

She'd run away from Richard too. Pen laid her head back on the armrest of her sofa and closed her eyes. The leaden weight in her chest had nothing to do with Lolita. She couldn't go on day after day with Richard anymore, knowing she exposed more and more of her gooey attraction to him. She doubted that she'd ever been more confused in her life. But the way he left that night with her honor intact had been humiliating. She was a mature woman who was supposed to be able to control her own physical actions. She hadn't then. In fact, she hadn't been doing it since Richard had showed up.

So she'd been cooped up in her house for the last few days. Richard never showed up to beg her to come back to the set, and oddly she resented him even more for that. Libby wisely didn't say a thing in her evening telephone calls. She only complained about Mary Jane.

Whatever was going on up there on the mountain, it was hot and heavy.

Opening her eyes, she reached over and got the remote control, clicking on the television. To her shock, Richard's face bloomed on the screen. His rare interview. Her brain told her fingers to press the buttons on the remote, but the message never got through. Richard stayed on the screen, and Pen's eyes were glued to him.

He slouched down in a comfortable-looking chair, his hair scraped back in a ponytail, a day-old stubble along his jaw. He looked unkempt, extremely pained to be where he was, and devastatingly sexy. He answered questions with one-word answers, never looked the interviewer in the eye, and his hands flailed around aimlessly while his knees rocked apart and together like a metronome. He had the classic signs of shyness in its glory, and Pen's heart went out to him.

"I understand you took a survival training course to prepare for this role," the interviewer said.

Richard straightened in the chair, then slouched again, looking away. "Yes."

Silence ensued, the interviewer clearly expecting Richard to elaborate and Richard just as clearly not.

"This movie is about a man torn between his white roots and his Indian upbringing, right?" the woman prompted.

Richard was quiet for a long moment. "That's right."

More silence.

"Oh, Lordy," Pen muttered, putting her hands over her face. How she ever got an entire lesson on tracking out of him . . .

"I also understand there's a bit of off-camera romance going on."

Pen immediately flipped open her hands. Richard reacted with lightning speed, sitting up, his body tense. And damning. Nothing else could have signaled the truth in the interviewer's statement better than that.

"Say no," Pen muttered, glaring at the screen. "No, no, no."

But a perverse little voice inside her wanted him to say yes, to make a public commitment.

Richard said nothing.

The interviewer grinned. "A little bird told me you and a lucky local schoolteacher are very chummy-chummy. So who is your new ladylove?"

"I thought this was supposed to be an interview about the movie," Richard said through a locked jaw. At least it looked locked, he was clenching it together so tightly.

"Oh, it is," the woman assured him, her expression like a gimlet skewering her victim. "I take it that the rumor's true."

"I never said it was true!" Richard snapped.

"Ah, but you haven't said it isn't."

Another dead silence. Pen groaned and covered her eyes again. Lolita got up and walked off her chest, clearly disgusted with the continual disturbance of their feline-human love fest.

"My personal life is of no concern—"

"Of course it is," the interviewer corrected, leaping

in. "Your fans want to know all about you, Richard. You're such a mystery man. But if you're in love, you don't want to be closemouthed, do you? You wouldn't want to disappoint your fans by keeping your own true love story a secret from them."

Pen held her breath, realizing that he could come off as a super prima donna, depending on what he said about the fans.

The expression on his face changed. "But if I tell everything, then I won't be a mystery man anymore."

"Good answer!" Pen exclaimed, sitting up.

The interviewer laughed. "I suppose that's true. But won't you at least tell us a little about this new love in your life?"

The interview went on like that for several more minutes, with Richard avoiding a direct answer and the interviewer pushing for it every step of the way.

The interview no sooner signed off than Pen's telephone rang. She snatched it up. It was Libby, who was apologizing for the leak on the set. She hung up and it rang again, her neighbor this time, asking if *she* was the local because Richard had been seen at her house. She hung up. It rang yet again, right under her hand.

Pen snatched her fingers away and stared at the telephone. Anger coalesced inside her. How could this have happened? And what about her job? A teacher's private life was private, but one never knew what a school board might take into its collective head. And her private life had just been on national TV! Richard Creighton, Mystery Man, was going to ruin her reputation in this town. She had to stop the potential for gossip this very minute.

She turned and headed for her front door.

The sudden pounding on his trailer door was so fierce that Richard wondered for an amused moment if it could knock the mobile home over on its side.

"Richard! You open this door this instant!" Pen shouted.

"She saw the show," he muttered, all his hopes shattered. "Okay, okay!"

The pounding stopped and he got the door open. Pen swept inside the trailer, demanding, "How could you?"

"How could I what?" he asked, stalling for time as he stepped outside and glanced at the trailer door for dents. It was too dark to see clearly, so he gave up until the morning.

"Richard!"

He turned around and came inside behind her, closing the door on his doom. She was wearing a tank top and camp shorts, her hair wild around her shoulders, as if she'd been pulling at it anxiously. She probably had. Still, it didn't hinder his automatic reaction to her. Pure lust. He cleared his throat. "I'm sorry, Pen, but that damn woman just sprang it on me—"

"Why didn't you just tell her the truth?" Pen asked, her arms folded across her chest in a defiant stance. The gesture pushed the upper curves of her breasts together in the most breathtaking manner. "Why didn't you deny the whole thing?"

Richard blinked. "But that would be a lie."

"Richard!" Pen flung herself around in a circle, clearly looking for room to pace. There wasn't any.

"Pen, calm down," he began, realizing she was furious with him. Why should she be furious with him? *He* didn't do anything wrong. "The show was taped this morning. We tried all day to get them to edit out that part, but they wouldn't. I'm on your side, remember?"

"Do you know what you've done?" she asked. "I bet it's already all over town. Soon it'll be all over the county. The school board might try to take my job from me."

"They can't!" Richard said, glaring at her. "That's ridiculous. You're a single woman, entitled to have your own life. I realize you're upset—"

"A lot you know." She ran her fingers through her loose hair in exasperation, causing the one side to stick practically straight up. "Richard, school boards are like kingdoms unto themselves. Oh, they might not fire me outright because people are gossiping about my love life, but they'll discuss it openly at meetings, concerned about my 'moral influence' on the children. The parents may get riled up in the process. Then they'll find some reason to get rid of me that even the union can't bust. Or they'll 'bow' to public opinion and not worry about any possible lawsuit I might file. You'd be surprised what can happen."

"But, Pen, you have no love life," Richard said logically.

"And why didn't you tell the woman that?" Pen shouted in his face.

Richard backed up. "I'm sorry, Pen. But how do you think I feel, having this thrown in my face on national TV? I'm entitled to as much privacy as anyone else. I hate doing interviews. I told you that before."

"You know what I think?" Pen asked. From the narrow-eyed expression on her face, Richard had a feeling he didn't want to know. She went on, unfortunately, answering her own question. "I think that whole interview was a nice publicity generator for Richard Creighton, actor."

"The hell it was!" Richard snapped. "I would never do something like that, Pen."

"You need to keep your name before the public," she reminded him. "Isn't gossip a perfect way to do so?"

"What the hell happened here?" he demanded, having had enough of all this nonsense. "I was the one made to look stupid. I was the one who was harassed by the interviewer, and you're blaming *me?*"

"Yes, I'm blaming you," Pen said. "If you had

handled it with a bit more finesse, you would have given the woman *nothing*."

"I'm sorry I'm too much of 'the Cretin' to suit you," he said stiffly.

Her eyes widened at his words. For one long, long moment, she just stared at him, then her expression collapsed. "Oh, Richard. I didn't mean for you to think that."

"What else am I supposed to think?" he asked, relaxing a little. "I acted like a cretin in that interview—unsophisticated, no finesse."

"Innocent enough not to dissemble." She shook her head. "I'm still angry as hell, but I suppose you couldn't help yourself."

"Gee, thanks," he muttered, shoving his hands in his shorts pockets. He glanced up. "What can I do to help you now?"

"Don't do any more interviews," she replied, and had the grace to chuckle.

"I promise." He gazed at her face, softened now, drinking in her features. "I've missed you."

She looked away for a moment. "How are things going on the set?"

He made a face. "Don't ask."

"That bad, eh?"

"Mary Jane definitely likes to stir things up," he said, shaking his head. He decided she probably didn't want to hear the particulars. "Let's just say that it's tense. Getting back to our problem, someone from the set is a leak. Probably that damned publicist. He arranged the interview, and insisted I do it. If it's any consolation, that interviewer will probably have trouble in the future finding other major actors who are willing to talk to her. She violated an unwritten rule about embarrassing actors in public."

"I'd like to thwack her," Pen muttered grimly. "And you."

He chuckled. "Can't I just wear a hair shirt for life?"

"Not good enough."

He felt, if not totally forgiven, at least reprieved. Taking a chance, he reached out and touched her bare arm. Her flesh was warm and silky. A haze clouded his vision, and heat flooded his own skin. He shouldn't, he thought. He'd promised to be a gentleman until she was ready to further the relationship. But he couldn't stay away.

"Pen," he whispered, drawing her to him.

"I . . . I can't," she said. "I shouldn't."

"Please. I need to touch you just once."

Her eyelids fluttered closed as if he caused her pain. Then she whispered, "Only once."

If there was any resistance now, he didn't sense it. She came into his arms as if made for them. Her body was solid and real, not like the phantoms of his restless bed. Her breasts pressed into his chest, and he turned up her chin, splaying his fingers across her cheek before bringing his mouth down on hers.

The kiss was filled with longing. He wanted her so badly; he'd missed her so much. The days had been unhappy and the nights pure torture. Yet he hadn't known how to break through the barrier she'd set up.

But now she'd come to him. In anger maybe, but he wasn't letting her go this time. He pulled her hard against him, his kiss almost bruising. Almost. Her mouth was yielding, and pumped his need for her higher. He ran his hands through her hair, the strands winding around his fingers. He could feel the delicate line of her jaw, the smooth warmth of her skin. The kiss went on and on until he was dizzy.

They were both gasping for breath when he finally lifted his head. He wanted to say something, to reassure her, to promise sincerely that he'd be a gentleman ... but the notions went straight out of his head the moment he looked at her flushed features and lidded gaze. They kissed again, their hands clinging seemingly everywhere at once as each tried to pull the other closer. He pressed his hips into hers, pushing her back against the refrigerator. He wrestled the bottom of her tank top up and pushed her bra down, exposing her breasts. With mouth and hands, he tasted and caressed, marveling at the incredible texture of her nipples against his tongue. She moaned and clung, her fingers clawing at his back and pulling at his hair. He felt so good, so solid and so right.

He wanted more of her. He needed to claim her as his own and damn what anybody would think.

Somehow they made it into the tiny bedroom, collapsing together on the cramped bunk. Her clothes seemed to stick to her body; he couldn't get them off easily. Either that, or his fingers were suddenly all thumbs. But buttons and zippers and clothing were finally dispensed with.

"You're beautiful," he murmured in awe, as she lay back on his bed. Her breasts were full and heavy from his touch, the nipples rosy and beckoning. Her small waist tapered to a taut stomach before flaring into feminine hips and lush thighs, her woman's flesh hidden, mysterious.

She ran her hands up his arms, her fingers digging in slightly, demanding him, wanting him. The message sang along his veins. He'd never wanted anyone before the way he wanted Pen.

He ran his hands along her thighs and upward, retracing the course of his gaze. Bending forward, he nuzzled her breasts over and over until she was frantic under him. He stroked her inner flesh, feeling her moistness, her need fueling his own, until he couldn't wait any longer. . . .

"Richard, do you . . . have anything?" she murmured in his ear.

He raised his head in bewilderment. "Any what? Oh."

He reached for the foil package in his wallet on

the tiny bureau, grateful she had remembered to protect them both. He had wanted to be prepared in case their relationship deepened as he'd hoped. No regrets, he thought, as her hands took over the small task, driving him wild in the process. He pushed her down on her back again, running his tongue once around her nipple. He kissed her neck and settled his hips into the cradle of her thighs.

"Richard . . ."

His name on her lips was an invitation, one he had been desperate to hear. He plunged into her softness, losing himself inside her as the most incredible feelings washed over him: want and need and satisfaction all at once. He forgot himself as the emotions culminated inside him in a rush of bliss. . . .

And then he realized how out of control he really was. He tried to stop himself but he couldn't, couldn't stop how he felt about her. Never had he wanted anyone as much as he wanted Pen—and it showed.

"I'm sorry," he muttered, his breath coming in sharp rasps. He felt like a stupid teenager with his first girl. "I wanted you so badly, Pen . . ."

"It's okay," she murmured back, caressing his shoulders in reassurance. "In fact, it's flattering that you want me so much. But next time, wait for me."

Relief washed over him. He chuckled and kissed the softness just under her ear. The scent of her swirled through the corners of his mind, drugging his senses.

His hand found her breast, the nipple springing to life under his palm.

"I think it's next time," he said, lifting his head and pressing his hips even deeper into hers.

"I can tell," she said, pulling his head down for her kiss.

This time he waited. He more than waited, as he took her time and again over the edge into the velvet darkness until the scent of her, the taste of her, the feel of her flesh sheathing his was so imprinted on his brain and body that she would live within him forever. And then, in the small bed that sheltered them, he went over the edge with her for the first time.

SEVEN

Pen became aware of a heavy weight across her stomach, her back against a solid wall. She tried to shift her body into a more comfortable position, but somehow couldn't manage to do so.

Then the night came flooding back to her.

Pen opened her eyes, hoping against hope she wouldn't see what she was afraid she'd see. She saw it. Wincing, she squeezed her eyelids tightly shut. The ceiling of the small trailer was barely visible in the first gray streaks of morning. Richard's trailer. Richard's arm was around her. Richard's naked body was against her own naked body. His skin was snuggled warmly along the length of her.

"Oh, boy," she muttered under her breath. How could she have done this? Where had her brain been? She'd certainly compromised their relationship now. And with people focused on both of them at the moment. She should have resisted his plea . . . and she knew she couldn't have. She'd wanted this as much as he did. One time. But now one time was over, and she had to face reality. She wondered if she could get out of the bed and out of the trailer without waking him. . . .

The alarm went off.

Pen shrieked, her body jumping automatically at the sudden sound. A large male hand reached out and smacked the top of the clock radio. The rest of the body never moved.

"Richard," she said, shaking him. Maybe it was better this way, she thought. The sooner he got up, the sooner she got out.

"I'm awake, Mom," he mumbled.

"Richard!" she exclaimed indignantly.

He opened his eyes wide, as if surprised by the voice next to him. Then his expression relaxed into a sleepy smile. "You're not Mom."

"Thank goodness." She nudged him while trying to pull the sheet up under her chin. Unfortunately, the material was trapped under his arm and would come no higher than the highest curves of her breasts. At least her nipples were decently covered. "Your alarm went off."

"Pen, do you regret this?" he asked, clearly sensing her distress.

She gazed at him, conscious of his body next to hers. He was raised on his elbow, concern showing in his eyes. His hair hung down on his shoulders, tousled and completely masculine. The darker hairs of his chest and forearms didn't begin to hide the lean, corded muscles. He looked wild and magnificent, and she wanted him all over again.

She sighed, the tension going out of her body with the gesture, and she told the truth. "I don't regret being with you. But it complicates things considerably, not to mention the bad timing."

He relaxed. "As long as you don't regret what happened. I don't want you to. Not ever. I know it complicates things—"

"More than you know." She managed a chuckle. "Come on, you better get moving, otherwise Libby will kill us both. What damn time does that thing go off, anyway?"

"Five-thirty."

She groaned. "My cousin is a torturer in disguise."

"It's normal hours, Pen, for actors." He was silent for a moment, not moving to get up. "Pen—"

"Richard." She reached out and touched his cheek, feeling the first bristles of his whiskers against her fingertips. "It's okay. Really."

He eyed her, then nodded. Leaning down, he kissed her softly until she melted under him. Then he kissed her again before saying, "You're sure?"

She nodded. "I'm sure."

He got out of bed, leaving the sheet across his middle until the very last moment, charmingly considerate of his nudity. Pen looked heavenward. Why couldn't he be a jerk, like anyone would expect an actor to be? But no, Richard had to do those innocent things that wormed their way into her heart. Lord help her, but he did.

She wondered how many of her neighbors knew she hadn't spent the night in her own home and how she was going to get back into it without being seen. And why the hell should she be worrying about it? Unfortunately, because if parents took it into their heads that she was immoral, it could mean her job. But Richard was emotionally vulnerable too.

She couldn't face it all, she thought in confusion. It was better to put her feelings away and take them out and examine them later, when she could look at them objectively.

She was dressed when he emerged from his dinky shower, a towel wrapped around his hips.

"Aren't you taking a shower?" he asked. The question was innocuous, but the panic in his gaze wasn't.

She rose to her feet and put her arms around him, pressing her cheek against his chest, feeling the coolness of his wet skin and the strength of his muscles underneath. It nearly undid her good intentions. She took a deep breath and forced her mind into control. "Richard, it's okay. You need to get to the location. I'll shower at my place, I promise." She stopped and laughed. "Do you realize that everyone thinks you're bathing in the local stream?"

"Too shallow." He shrugged dismissively, clearly in no mood for humor. "Can I see you tonight,
Pen?"

She knew she ought to tell him no, that she really
couldn't see him, not only for her own sanity, but also
to keep her job. But the only thought in her brain
was not to hurt him. And he *was* hurt. Ironic, she
thought. Usually the woman felt hurt and neglected
the morning after. Not the man.

One more plus in Richard's corner to bring her
down.

"Yes," she murmured. "I'll come by here after
you're done shooting for the day."

"Good."

She could hear the pleasure in his voice, and that
pleased her. Their leave-taking almost didn't take, the
good-bye kiss nearly undoing both their good intentions. But she managed to get out the trailer door and
down the mountainside without incident.

The sun was only inches above the horizon when
she turned down her street. A group of unfamiliar
vehicles were parked along the curb in front of her
house, several people leaning against them while chat-
ting with each other. Cameras were slung around one
or two necks.

Paparazzi.

All hell had broken loose.

❦———————❦

Richard found himself surrounded by a large group of tabloid stringers after he parked his truck on the location site. He pushed his way past them without a word, grateful that Pen wasn't with him this morning. He had to admit he was now glad that she wasn't coming to the set.

"What the hell is this?" he demanded of Libby as soon as he reached her.

"Your adoring fans," she replied sarcastically.

"Where's security?" he asked, furious. "Why aren't they keeping those people down at the base of the mountain?"

"Security is on its way," Libby said. "They weren't expecting this. None of us was."

"I need to call Pen," he said. "She's suppose to come over tonight, but those people will follow me back to the trailer."

Libby shook her head. "All we've got are cellular phones here. People are probably already monitoring the bands. Unless you want the world to know you're planning to come back as someone's knickers, better forget using them."

Richard cursed.

"Better hang on to that one," Libby said. "I've got more bad news. About your trailer—"

"My trailer!" Richard burst out, his first thought that someone had already discovered Pen had been there through the night. "What about my trailer?"

"You can't go back there," Libby said. "The

reporters are bound to follow you, and if they take pictures . . . they can make it look bad for the studio and the movie and you, like nobody's treating you right or you're off your rocker. The studio has a house for you. A very fancy one, all cedar and glass, and it's off by itself on thirty-five acres. They want you to use it."

"But I don't want to use it."

Libby raised her eyebrows meaningfully. "I don't think it's a request. I'm having your stuff moved over this morning per studio orders."

He couldn't believe it, couldn't believe any of this. "Dammit, why is my personal life suddenly everybody's business?"

"Because you are an actor's actor who's always been squeaky-clean, and now there's some dirt. It's far more interesting to speculate on Mr. Goody Two-Shoes' having an affair than to print another Liz-goes-on-a-diet piece. You're hot right now and that makes you news. Besides, what are you doing with my cousin anyway?"

He glared at her. Libby glared back.

"Just be careful with her," Libby said. "She's not as tough as she seems. And I didn't bring you into this movie for you to test your newfound stud image on my cousin."

"I'm not testing *anything* on Pen," he snapped, furious with Libby.

"Fine. I'll get a message to her about the problems at your place—"

"Good morning, all!"

Mary Jane's chipper voice broke up Richard and Libby's conversation. He turned to face his costar, finding her disgustingly cheerful.

"Richard, Richard." She pinched his cheek in mock affection. "We haven't even started yet, and you're looking glum. Don't let all this hoopla get you down. I thought you did a good job on that interview—as good as you were capable of doing. So what are we talking about here? The motivation for the upcoming scene? I really don't like this scene, Libby. I come off as very calculating—"

"Calculating!" Libby gasped. "You only ask Richard if he wants more stew as he talks with your husband about the wisdom of sending men out of the fort."

"It's not right for me," Mary Jane insisted. "Maybe I should be the one talking to my husband about the men, rather than Richard. . . ."

Richard gritted his teeth. From the moment he'd awakened this morning, nothing had gone right.

At the end of a long, exhausting day of fighting Mary Jane over scenes and ducking reporters, Richard arrived at his new home. He walked through the cedar-and-glass rooms and desperately wished he could go back to his trailer. This was too sterile and luxurious to suit him. But it did have one good thing: a telephone with blessed, secure lines. He put his hand on the receiver, then remembered about wiretapping. How far would a tabloid go?

He cursed at the very possible answer. Damn! How was he supposed to get in touch with Pen? How could he know she was okay? He couldn't, not if he cared about her. What they plastered all over their front pages about him didn't matter. But if they said one word about Pen . . . worse, if he contributed to that. He had been hurt by her that morning, but now he understood her concerns. He wanted to be with her, to tell her things, intimate things, important things.

But he couldn't go near her. Not yet.

"Damn you, Richard Creighton."

Pen huddled behind some trash cans as she watched the reporters clustered at the foot of her walkway. She'd tried all day to get near the place, but reporters were all over it, front and back, every time she'd driven by. She'd gone to the set to see Libby and had found reporters staked out there as well. Then she'd gone back to Richard's trailer only to discover it had vanished! She'd spent the day in her car, going back and forth from the local pizza shop to her house.

Now it was evening and some of the reporters had finally given up. She'd planned to sneak into her house by going through the yards across the back, but now she was holed up behind the Stonemans' trash cans. So far they hadn't looked out their side window and caught her. So far.

How had the reporters found out about her? She'd love to know who had squealed—and kill the informer! She wondered if anyone else knew what it was like to spend the day in the Twilight Zone. She'd unwittingly contributed to this kind of frenzy in the past by being just as curious as anyone else about celebrity gossip. Oh, she didn't buy the tabloids and would never admit her interest to anyone, but she did read every bit of the blaring headlines at the supermarket checkout counter. She took delight along with the majority of the public in the naughtiest ones. *Never again.* Charles and Di could have a fistfight in Paddington Station, and she wouldn't even look at the front page photo. Not after this!

If only she could have forced herself to stroll up her walkway in a brazen manner . . .

Cameras would have gone off right on the spot, ruining with their eventual headlines whatever reputation she had. And the irony was that only yesterday the headlines would have been totally false. She couldn't risk it. Poor Lolita had probably eaten all her dry food and was desperate for her overdue meal. She *had* to get in that house!

Action came faster than she anticipated when she heard Joe Stoneman's voice on the other side of the wall. That he was murmuring sweet nothings to his wife in loud enough tones for New York City to hear was the deciding factor. Three was definitely company. Pen scooted on her bottom out from behind the trash cans and along the grass lawn. She felt like a crab with a hernia problem. She made it to her house without being spotted, the reporters more involved with their dinner than their quarry. Brutus, the local watchdog, barked a couple of times, but he barked at everything. The reporters were probably used to it by now.

"Remind me never to go crazy over a movie star again," she muttered as she let herself in the back door.

Lolita greeted her with loud plaintive cries. Pen resisted the urge to turn on the lights, instead fumbling in the dark with cat food cans and the electric opener. Lolita was pacified finally, and Pen pressed the button to hear the calls on her answering machine. The first was from Libby, telling her not to go to Richard's trailer.

"No kidding," she muttered, then clamped her jaw on complaints when Libby added that she should stay off the telephone and definitely not call certain people.

This was ridiculous, she thought in disgust, but didn't boldly turn lights on and run around banging pots and pans together.

After that the calls were from reporters giving numbers for her to return calls, interspersed with more from local people who seemed to have divined that she was the mysterious woman in Richard's life. What was this? Psychictown, U.S.A.?

But one call was missing. From Richard. She knew what she'd said that morning, but she would have thought he would have at least called. The disappointment in her heart should have surprised her. But it didn't. . . .

She became aware of a soft tapping on a kitchen window. Her stomach tightened and a vision of a rabid reporter à la Hitchcock going on a blood rampage ran through her brain.

She shook herself. "Get a grip!"

Still, she was cautious as she approached the back door.

"Pen?" said a male voice. "Pen, are you there? Let me in if you are."

"Richard!" she gasped, and flung the door open.

He slipped inside.

"Are you crazy?" she demanded, the darkness obscuring his face. She pulled him down into a crouch beside the door, not wanting anyone to see one, let alone two, human shadows in the windows. "This is not the time to think you're James Bond, dammit. Those reporters would have a field day if they knew you were here!"

"I know, but I wanted to make sure you were all right." He stared at her. "*Are* you all right?"

"I've spent the entire day trying to get into my own house. I'm tired, I'm hungry, I'm sick of pizza, and I'm so mad I'm ready to spit." She smiled sweetly. "But other than that, it's been a hunky-dory day. Now get the hell out of here before anyone sees you. If they haven't already!"

"It's okay," he said. "I was very careful."

She knew he had the training to fade in and out without being seen, but that didn't ease her panic. Even if he hadn't been seen coming in, he could be seen leaving.

"I'm sorry about all this," Richard said. "This isn't the kind of romantic aftermath I had in mind."

"It's not your fault," she said. And it wasn't. It was hers for getting involved with him in the first place. "By the way, you've vanished off the face of the mountain, or at least your trailer isn't there anymore."

"You went back? Didn't you get Libby's message?"

"Just now on the answering machine," she said. "I haven't been able to get near the house all day so I thought I'd try your trailer again. Where the heck is it, anyway?"

"Nowhere." His voice turned sarcastic. "The studio *requested* I move into a house. Ordered is more like it. I'm in some cedar-and-glass thing off Route 602 in Franklin Grove."

"Cedar and glass? Set way off the road on several acres?"

He nodded.

"That's owned by the head of Dow Corning. It's his summer home. Or else it's Joe Papp's old place."

"Dow Corning owns a piece of the studio," Richard said.

"Then that's probably the one." Pen leaned back against her door and closed her eyes, exhausted. Wanting nothing more than a shower and bed, she swallowed against the lump of tears clogging her throat, knowing she might unconsciously follow habit and flip on a light switch, thereby alerting the hounds outside that she was in. "I can't use my phone, so Libby says. I can't take a shower. I can't sleep. I can't leave my house. I can't live like this! How long is this going to go on?"

"I'm sorry, Pen," Richard said, settling down next to her. He put his arm around her, and to her own surprise, she didn't push him away.

She felt grungy and wished she were at her best rather than like this, but he didn't seem to mind or even notice. She leaned against his chest, needing the comfort and warmth of another human being, this human being, above all else.

"Is there any way to get rid of them?" she asked.

"I don't know." He was silent for a long moment. "I do know you're right, though. You can't live like this."

She managed a chuckle. "They would kill to know you were in here with me."

He laughed. "Shall I go open the front door and say hi?"

"Oh, absolutely. Then after that we can run naked through the streets."

"Works for me."

Lolita mewed plaintively and crawled up onto their legs. Now that she was fed, she clearly wanted affection.

"Maybe we ought to send the cat out there," Richard said. "She'd give Socks a run for his money."

Pen straightened as an idea hit her smack between the eyes. "Brutus! Why didn't I think of him earlier?"

"Who's Brutus?" Richard asked.

"A lovely big monster of a dog who lives two doors down. Brutus doesn't like strangers. He doesn't bite them, he just doesn't like them. I think the reporters would love to meet him, don't you?"

Richard laughed. "I'm sure it will be a spectacular interview. Did anyone ever tell you you're a wicked person, Pen?"

"My class, every time I assign homework for the weekend." She grinned. "You stay here. I'll be right back."

"But—"

"But what?" she interrupted. "You can't go out with me. Brutus will alert five counties that you're here."

"So he was the one who was barking when I came through the back," Richard said. "He only barked once, though."

Pen smiled. She slipped out the back door, her heart stopping for an instant when the men in front laughed at some joke. Brutus barked a couple of times when she neared his doghouse, but, recognizing her voice, quieted when she called softly to him.

Despite his name, Brutus wasn't a vicious dog, only a big, dumb, happy, half Irish wolfhound, half Saint Bernard who loved to chase anything that moved, then tree it. He got loose sometimes from his chain, mostly because none lasted long against his strength, and usually proceeded to corner a local cat or the mailman. And he would keep them there forever if he could. Even the mailman's Mace never stopped him. Brutus had the patience and determination of Joan of Arc. Pen grinned, knowing she could depend on Brutus.

As soon as she got within doggy reach, Brutus knocked her on her back and licked her face, his heavy body pinning her on the ground and nearly killing her in the process. The tail and hindquarters swished madly from side to side in his joy. It was like being under an enormous car wash. Pen finally managed to push the dog off her, rubbing at her now-wet face. Kisses sweeter than wine were not Brutus's forte. She got the chain unhooked, grabbed onto the leather collar, and led him in the direction of her house. Rather, Brutus bounded, dragging her along. At least he was going the right way. But the moment they crossed the yard in between, the large square head came up at the sound of strange voices and the smell of new scents. Pen snatched her fingers out from under the collar in the split second before Brutus bayed and zoomed down the small grass alley between the houses, dead on his target.

Pen watched him go. Sure enough, the massive body of Saint Bernard ancestry and the wiry gray coat of the wolfhound had its usual Hound-from-Hell effect. The intrepid reporters scattered in panic as Brutus broke into the open. They ran as one for their cars, making it inside the vehicles with nanoseconds to spare. All but one. The poor soul banged on the window, but the comrade inside refused to take a chance and unlock the car door for him. He spun around several times, then leaped onto the roof of the car. Brutus, not being the brightest of God's good creatures, tried to jump straight up from the side of the car, rather than go up the easy way over the hood or trunk. He missed by inches, falling back to the ground. But there was no doubt in anyone's mind that he'd eventually figure the puzzle out, one way or another, and, if not, that he'd become a canine battering ram. Engines started, and cars, one by one, like beads on a chain, pulled out from the curb and roared down the street, the driver of the one with the reporter still clinging to the roof going more slowly than his fellows. Baying loudly the entire time, Brutus raced after them, determined as always to catch his new toys.

"Ahh," Pen sighed. "Life is good."

She hurried the last few feet to her house as lights came on and doors opened, people curious about the sudden noises. Richard already had the door open, and she collapsed over the threshold, laughing. Richard pulled her into his arms, hugging her in delight.

"Did you see?" she asked, wiping at tears. "They couldn't get in their cars fast enough."

"I saw," he said, amused. "There are a lot of people in Hollywood who would have loved to have seen it too. I wish I'd videotaped it."

"Too bad Libby wasn't here," Pen said. "She would have called for a second take."

"Now that would have been something to see." He sniffed at the air. "You smell peculiar."

"It's eau de Brutus." She sniffed herself. "And lack of a shower."

"I told you you should have taken one this morning."

She disentangled herself from his arms, remembering full well why she hadn't. "You were right."

"At last." He didn't seem at all to feel her pulling away was a rejection of him. She was glad, because it hadn't been.

Richard's demeanor got serious. "Pen, you can't stay here. The dog won't keep them away forever. They'll be back, and they'll be pounding down your doors. You have to go now while you can."

"But I can't!" she exclaimed. "This is my house. Besides, who would feed Lolita?"

"We'll take her with us."

"We?" Pen echoed.

"We," Richard said firmly. "You'll go with me now, tonight. Then we'll figure out what to do with you tomorrow."

"I can't go with you! They'll be expecting us to be together."

"But they don't know where I am, remember?" He scooped up Lolita, then said, "Get some clothes. Now."

"Richard," Pen began, although she was leery of the stern tone in his voice. Richard had never been stern.

"Dammit, Pen!" He towered over her, glaring. "I'm not arguing with you. You either get your clothes or we go now without them. Use your brain. You know you can't stay here. This is your one chance to go, and you're going."

She knew he was right. But to go with him was to risk everything. Yet to not go was to ensure they'd have a printable picture of her before two days were out.

She went and got her clothes.

As he lay back in his bed, fully dressed, Richard tried to ignore the woman in his shower. His nice, big shower with room for two.

They had gotten to his new hideaway without

incident. No cars had followed and none were near the property or road. So far this hadn't leaked, he thought. So far. He hoped that they'd decide there was no truth to the rumor and give up, or that another, far more juicy rumor would require their follow-up.

If ever there was a man who stumbled through relationships, it was he. This time he'd hit a doozy. How could Pen want him after this? She couldn't—and he couldn't blame her, either. The morning after should bring two people even closer together, not create disaster.

Lolita snuggled up against his side, purring loudly, clearly happy in her new home. He sighed and put his arm around her.

"Wrong female, sweetheart," he murmured. "But I love you too."

It was the "too" that made him pause. He knew Pen had gotten under his skin, right from the beginning. But love . . .

He heard the fan light click off and the bathroom door open, and he immediately leaped from the bed, sending poor Lolita yowling and scrambling away in fright. He'd been very careful earlier not to make any overtly sexual moves, unsure of his reception, and he didn't want to start now.

Pen emerged. Her hair was damp and she was dressed in a thin cotton nightgown and robe. "Oh!" she said, startled.

"You can have this room," Richard said, not able to lift his gaze from her slender curves. "I . . . I wanted to tell you that."

"But this is the master bedroom," she protested. "It was enough that I used the shower, which you really didn't have to insist on."

"Its windows face the back of the property. The other ones face the road. Just a precaution." He wondered how to overcome this awkwardness between them. Granted, the events of the day would put a dent in even the strongest relationship, but it didn't even allow a chance for theirs.

"I suppose you're right," she conceded.

"Well . . . good night." He wished he could become somebody, grab up a character's veneer for a moment, but nothing came to mind. He had to be honestly himself.

He turned away.

"Richard?"

He turned back. "Yes?"

"Stay with me."

He gaped at her, shocked that she still wanted him. Then he realized that being honestly himself was enough. More than enough.

He stopped gaping and went to her.

EIGHT

The solution to her problem, when it arrived, was an easy one. But it wasn't the one she wanted.

"There," Libby said, with a satisfied finality. "All settled in my guest room. What's more natural than two cousins sharing a house?"

"Pigs flying?" Pen asked. She stuffed some of her clothes in the drawer. Lolita was sprawled on the bed in feline splendor.

"It works," Richard said. "Who's looking at what Libby's doing?"

"The finance men," Libby muttered. "But we won't get into that."

Pen smiled ruefully at Richard. He and Libby had cooked this up between them on the set, the only two who knew where she was. He had brought her under the cover of night, after she had spent the day chafing in the chairman of the board's house. The place had been a sterile museum, with not one expensive collector's item out of place. It all made her itch to get away from it. But leaving Richard behind was torture. He was the only reason to stay. A very powerful one, she admitted.

She was thoroughly hooked. The moment he'd turned to leave that perfect bedroom last night, she had collapsed emotionally, knowing if he were down the hallway all night long, it would be impossible. She'd wanted him, wanted the comfort and the passion he offered. She knew the opportunity would be gone with the morning.

And morning had come, a different one from the day before. Instead of being strained with each other, they had made a complete commitment to working together to get out of the tangle they were in. She might not be as sure that Libby was the ultimate solution to throwing reporters off the trail, but no one had come up with a better one. All she knew was that she wanted to be with Richard.

"At least he can visit," Libby said, as if reading her thoughts.

"You only want to keep your star happy until the movie's done," Pen retorted with a grin.

"Well, I'm no saint." Libby turned to Richard. "I'll leave you alone with the prisoner for a few minutes, and then you better get going. Damn, what those clowns would pay me to know you two were here."

She left the room, chuckling. Richard pulled Pen into his embrace. She put her arms around his waist and laid her head on his chest.

"I do feel like a prisoner," she admitted, then shuddered. "With Libby as a jailer, Lord help me."

"It's a natural."

"What would be more natural would be Libby living at my house, not my living on the other side of town," Pen said.

"Libby's Hollywood; Libby's eccentric," Richard countered. "Libby has meetings and work that she can't very well impose on you, so she's rented her own home. But the two of you are family, so you move in here so you can visit until the filming's over. No one will think it odd, because Libby *is* odd. No one on the set knows you're here, so our leak can't give over that information to the media. And if they do, what will it prove? Nothing."

"We hope."

His arms tightened around her. "It's either this or be spread all over the front pages. Or leave town altogether."

"I don't want to do that." She lifted her face for his kiss.

When he left finally, Pen sat down on the bed, feeling as if she'd been in a tornado. Two days ago life had been normal. And now . . .

Libby came into her bedroom.

"He left," she said, smiling. "It's not so bad."

Pen eyed her sourly. "It's not so good."

"You make me sound like Jabba the Hutt."

Pen refrained from telling her cousin she looked like Jabba the Hutt, all big and smug. Libby wouldn't appreciate it.

"You've got it bad for him, don't you?" Libby asked, sitting down next to her.

Pen sighed. "That's the understatement of the year, Lib. The worst part is, I'm his filming fling and I know it and I don't care. He's . . . different."

"Richard in Hollywood is like a lamb wandering around in a den of lions. He's all naiveté, and they'll slaughter him for it. There are some actors who are great because they *don't* know all the facets of humanity; they discover them on camera. Richard's one of those. He needs someone like you, Pen, to keep him safe."

"I don't think I can," she said. "I'm not cut out for the fishbowl existence."

"I don't know." Libby chuckled. "You handled those reporters very well, letting that dog out after them. I wish I'd seen it."

Pen grinned. "It was beautiful."

"See? You can handle this. Piece of cake for you." Libby put her arm around her, giving her a fortifying hug. "Give it a week and they'll be gone. I promise."

"I'll hold you to it."

And Pen meant it.

As Richard climbed the back stairs of Libby's veranda, he couldn't believe the media people were still hanging around after a week. Not as many, but clearly the most tenacious stringers. Not even a rumor that Julia Roberts was coming out of seclusion had moved them. Five or six of them were always at the set in the morning, then following him home. Or trying to. Libby had set up several decoys for the ride back to his place, or he had been stored in the back of her trunk. But the maneuvering was getting more and more elaborate. And Pen was still cooped up at Libby's.

Why would they hang around still? Richard had a feeling the answer was that someone was telling them to. But who? If he had that answer, he'd have this problem all but solved.

Libby flung open the back door when he knocked on it. "What are you doing here? Did anyone see you? Are you crazy? I've got half the cast and crew coming over for a meeting! In fifteen minutes!"

"Why didn't I know about it?" he demanded, striding over the threshold and slamming the door shut behind him. "And are you crazy? Pen's here."

"I know Pen's here," Libby snapped, glaring at him. "She's staying in her room like a little mouse. And the reason you don't know about the meeting is because it's over Mary Jane's wardrobe. She hates it. Claudia, the wardrobe mistress, agrees. Claudia would."

Richard looked heavenward, grateful Libby hadn't told him. He wanted no part of it. "The producers got Jerry Osborne to design the costumes. He took great pains to use fabrics and styles that are historically accurate. She's already got the biggest and best American designer on the job, so what the hell does she want?"

"*Dangerous Liaisons on the Frontier.*" Libby waved her hands. "Will you get out of here!"

Suddenly he'd had enough of all the nonsense. He'd come to visit Pen, and he was damned well going to do that, meeting or no meeting.

"Okay." He headed directly for her inside stairs.

"What are you doing?" Libby squawked.

He smiled. "I'll hide with Pen until they're gone."

"You really are crazy!"

"We'll be quiet as church mice. I promise."

Libby's front doorbell rang, forestalling any further argument. Richard raced up the staircase and down the hall to Pen's room. He flung open the door.

"Wha . . . ?" She gaped at him, half rising from the bed. Dressed in shorts and top, she had dropped a book in her panic. Obviously she'd been settled in for a good read . . . until he'd shown up.

He put his finger to his lips while pointing toward the floor. Voices greeting each other drifted into the room. Pen's eyes widened. Richard smiled and shut the door, turning the lock behind him. He went over to her, then leaned down and kissed her still-open mouth.

That seemed to galvanize her to action. She whispered fiercely, "What are you doing here?"

"I came to visit," he whispered back.

"But Libby's having a meeting! You can't be here!"

"Well, I am. Scoot over." He nudged her over on the bed, then stretched out on the mattress. "Not bad. I think we'll survive."

"Who are we this time?" Pen asked.

"That was a very good play. Off-Broadway, I believe." He grinned. "I'm just me, tired of being always unsure of myself and away from you." And he was, he thought. Damn tired of the whole thing and refusing to let it run his life anymore. "I missed you."

She sighed. "I missed you too. But I have a feeling Ezekiel went over the cliff again."

"Nope. He's been sitting in a hut with ten men, planning for the fort's survival."

"The body fumes must have overwhelmed your brains."

"Very funny."

"Keep your voice down."

"Okay." He turned his whole body toward her and put his hand on her stomach, feeling the soft feminine muscles tense slightly at his touch. He kissed her arm. "There's only one way I know for us to be quiet." He kissed her shoulder, her collarbone, her throat, tasting the satin flesh exposed by the curve of her top. The scent of her, clean and sweet, pervaded his being, making him mindless to everything else.

"Richard." Her voice was slightly breathy. "We can't."

"It'd be interesting to see if two people could make love without making a sound." The thought of him making love to her while a houseful of people were downstairs was only all the more exciting.

"Without a single sound?" she asked, reaching up to toy with his hair. Her fingers threaded through the strands, tugging slightly and nearly undoing his control.

"Mmmm . . . think of it as a science experiment." He kissed the corner of her mouth. "We'll have to have a lot of tests."

"A lot."

She pulled his mouth down to hers.

Richard lay half atop Pen, contentedly reveling in the feel of her skin, soft yet vibrant, against his. One of his legs was between hers.

She was awake and playing with his hair, braiding the strands, then pressing her fingertips into them to undo the braids. "I love playing with your hair. It was a big mistake when short hair came back into fashion."

"I love playing with you," he said, pressing his hips into the side of her thigh.

"Ah, is this experiment number two?" she whispered, amusement in her tone.

"Eventually."

He liked this, lying with her in a cocoon of their own making. The voices from downstairs were faint, just on the edge of awareness. He smiled, thinking about what they would say if they knew what was going on right over their heads. The thought should make him panic, but it didn't.

"What?" Pen asked. "What's so funny?"

He raised his head. "How did you know I was amused?"

"I could feel you grinning against my shoulder."

"Oh. I was thinking about what everyone downstairs would say if they knew what was going on up here."

"No big deal," she replied, trailing her fingers along his shoulder blade. His skin twitched at the sensations she left behind. "We'd tell them it's a science experiment that failed."

"It was only the first test." He chuckled and lifted himself fully on top of her. "We'll improve with practice."

"Promise?"

"Absolutely."

Much later, after the voices had long stopped, a soft tapping sounded on the door. Libby called out, "They're gone."

"Good! Go 'way," Richard shouted, then gasped as Pen wrapped her legs around him, pulling him into her so deeply that he had to grit his teeth against crying out at the pleasure of it.

Pen did cry out, taking her with him over the brink, everything forgotten but the two of them together.

When Richard woke the next morning, the sun was well up in the sky. He knew he was late.

"Damn!" he cursed, flinging back the sheets and reaching around the floor for his briefs.

"What?" Pen mumbled sleepily. She looked all tousled, and he couldn't resist taking a moment to kiss her cheek. She smelled of perfume and the musky scent of her skin and his mingled together.

"It's after seven, and I'm supposed to be on the set at eight," he said, forcing himself to straighten.

She sat up. "After seven! Richard, you should have left ages ago."

He grinned wryly. "I fell asleep. What can I tell you? It must have been the company."

"Well, why didn't Libby wake us? She's up early, usually well before six."

"I don't know, but we'll damn well find out."

He hustled into his clothes while she threw on a robe, and they went downstairs together. Libby was gone. A note was propped on the kitchen table.

I tried to wake you earlier, about five—not to mention trying to get you out last night— but nobody was moving in there. Did you take Mickey Finns or something? Hope you had a . . . delightful visit and are feeling very pleased with yourselves. Richard, don't be late for work. AND DON'T SCREW UP LIKE THIS AGAIN!

"Great!" Pen said. "My cousin would break down the President's door if she thought he'd be late for the Oval Office. But today she gives up and strolls off to work."

"I've got to get out of here," Richard said. He kissed her soundly, then strode for the back door. His hand was actually turning the knob when he caught sight of the next-door neighbor watering her side garden. He cursed under his breath. "I can't go out that way."

"And you certainly can't go out the front," Pen told him.

"I know that!" He felt helpless, not able to come up with any solution on how to get out without being spotted and causing questions. A wild idea came to mind. "I need a dress."

Pen gaped at him.

"I need a dress," he said firmly, taking her hand and dragging her back up the stairs. "Only women live here, so only a woman can walk out without arousing suspicion. I need a dress. I only hope there's one that fits me."

"Richard . . ." She started laughing. "This is the most bizarre morning after we've had yet."

"Think of it as a tradition."

"I'm thinking of your masculinity if anyone catches on."

"That's not funny." He shrugged. "My masculinity will have to lump it. Got anything in a calf-length? I don't think I could get away with a mini. And I'll be damned to hell and back before I shave my legs!"

Pen burst into laughter.

Fifteen minutes later tears of mirth were streaming down her face as she planted a wide-brimmed straw hat on his head. "You never looked lovelier, Richard."

"Ha, ha, very funny." He made a face as he examined himself in the mirror. The long dress they'd found was like an iron lung at the chest, while the skirt flared out around his legs, leaving plenty of room for his rolled-up jeans underneath. "You don't think it's too tight across the top?"

Pen snorted in amusement. "You don't have a choice."

"True. Good thing Libby had one hat at least." He pulled the hat down low over his eyes. They'd left his hair unbound, Pen saying it looked "womanly." It had the advantage of hiding most of his face. His male ego was taking more than a beating, he admitted. A major death wish was more like it. "I look exactly like what I am. A guy in a dress."

"Keep your shoulders hunched over and your head down," Pen advised. "You only have to walk to the corner, only two houses down, and then to your car. You're an actor, so act. Jack Lemmon was great in *Some Like It Hot.*"

"Marilyn was better." He chuckled. "I'll act, don't worry. For someone who didn't think this would work, you're certainly for it now."

"I'm thinking positive."

He looked back at himself in the mirror, then shuddered. "I'm the Cretin all over again, only worse."

Pen wrapped her arms around him. "You've never been the Cretin, Richard. That was the other kids' problem, not yours. You look . . . sexy."

"How kind of you . . . really." He was grateful to her. "This had better work, otherwise I'll never live this down."

"If you think something will fail, you will help it along to doom," Pen said sternly, coming out of his embrace. "You *are* going to walk right out of here under everybody's nose and get away with it."

"I'll need an Academy Award performance," Richard said, and pulled her back into his arms. He kissed her lingeringly.

"I've never been kissed by a man in a dress before," Pen murmured when he finally lifted his head.

"Another first. And last." He examined himself one final time in the mirror, shuddered, then took a deep breath. "Okay, it's showtime."

The moment he opened the front door, he tried to put himself in Pen's shoes to make himself physically and emotionally into the woman he had to play. He visualized how she would walk down the porch steps and along the streets, what her expression would be, how she would be feeling inside. He didn't rush the process, keeping himself to a natural pace, not striding or clumping, but walking with the grace he admired in her. They had rounded out his outfit with a sweater to cover his arms and a shoulder bag with his shirt stuffed into it. The shoes he could do nothing about, Pen's and Libby's feet being too small, but his Docksiders were fine. He knew he looked very much like an Annie Hall yuppie, and in an upscale college town that was a common enough sight. He even waved to a woman across the street who had emerged to get her morning paper. She smiled and waved back.

He turned the corner in due course and spotted his Bronco. As he got into the driver's side, he heard and felt a rip under his outstretched right arm. The dress had had enough of him. More than enough. Still, he sighed in relief that he'd made it.

This second street was fairly deserted, only one person visible at the top of the hill. He didn't bother to wave to the man, instead starting the car. He deliberately made a U-turn to go back down Libby's street, right past the house. He hoped Pen was looking so she'd know he made it okay.

If anyone ever did a remake of *Charley's Aunt*, he was a shoo-in for the part.

But this nonsense had to stop, he thought. It absolutely had to stop.

"He really left dressed as a woman?" Libby laughed merrily, swiping at tears of amusement.

Pen glared at her cousin across the dinner table. "What else was he supposed to do? *You* didn't wake him up."

"I tried! I knocked on that door several times. You two were dead to the world. He never should have been there in the first place, let alone doing what you were doing. What if someone heard you and decided to investigate? Do you know how hard it was to keep everyone downstairs? I had to tell them the upstairs bathroom was clogged so they wouldn't use it. Mary Jane wanted to send over one of the set's techs to fix it. So don't tell me I was the one playing with fire. You and Richard were. An inferno, for heaven's sake!"

Pen could feel the heat saturating her cheeks. She could only wonder what Libby had seen when she'd opened the bedroom door. "Okay. But you don't have to laugh about it. How . . . how were things on the set?"

"Tense." Libby shook her head. "Mary Jane pretty much lost the argument over costuming, and she's on a rampage. It wouldn't have mattered if she'd won, though. She's continually disruptive, and she uses sit-down strikes like a dentist uses a drill—with about the same effect on the victims. I have to say she and Richard are creating the right kind of chemistry on-screen, though."

"They are?" Pen echoed, alarm bells going off inside her. "I thought he didn't like her."

"He doesn't. Oh, outwardly he tolerates her. But I think he's ready to kill her. That emotional tension translates itself into the kind of sexual tension their characters require."

Sexual tension. Something of the panic Pen was feeling must have shown on her face, because Libby said hastily, "He doesn't feel anything for her in real life, Pen. Except maybe disgust. It's simply that actors have this ability to turn their real feelings aside or into something that they can use in their acting. There're lots of incidences where actors who come across as sizzling on-screen really couldn't stand each other in real life."

"There're also lots of incidences where actors carried the parts too far. Liz and Dick. Tom Cruise and Nicole Kidman." Pen smiled bleakly. "I don't think I'm cut out for all this."

"Okay, so it happens sometimes. It's not happening now." Libby leaned forward. "I think it would be good for you to be on the set again."

"Are you crazy?" Pen jumped up and paced the kitchen. "I can't even move out of your house! I feel like a lion all caged up in a little bitty pen with the door wide open. I see it. I want to go through it. But I know I can't! So how can I go on the set? Those reporters are still out there."

"Nonetheless, I think it would be good for you to be on the set," Libby said stubbornly. "You'll shake up Mary Jane."

"I don't want to shake up Mary Jane! You're the director. You're the one who should control Mary Jane. If she's being a bad girl, put her in a corner."

Libby shook her head. "My job is to keep the stars happy. Because if the stars aren't happy, then they walk, and if they walk, the studio loses millions on the movie. The stars know it too. I can be controlling only to a certain point. I'd kill for the old studio contracts that kept people in line."

"Spoken like true management." Pen couldn't help feeling sympathetic to her cousin, despite her attitude. It was Libby's responsibility to get the movie made on time and on budget. The job was monumental, so Libby's twisted concern was understandable. "But no thanks on the subject of Mary Jane. I certainly don't want to tangle with her. One meeting was more than enough."

"Chicken."

"You're a bright woman, Libby." Pen winked. "Okay, so I'm sucking up. But you can undermine someone like Mary Jane, make her look foolish in subtle ways and take back control of the set. You run this picture. Mary Jane does not."

Libby sat back and sighed. "So I tell myself. I suppose I can't blame you for not wanting a part of it."

"Gee, thanks."

"You're welcome. But be careful with Richard! You and he don't want this blowing up in your faces over a foolish move! You've both worked too hard for that."

But as Pen cleaned up the dishes, for lack of anything else to do, she wondered if she could be wrong about not brazening things out. Pen dismissed the temptation to follow her advice to Libby to be bold and assertive. She'd stay put for a while longer. Even if she weren't concerned for her job's future, she certainly didn't want her name and picture plastered in the papers. She wished she could talk to Richard, see him, be with him most of the time.

Well, she thought, with them separated the way they were, she'd at least know if what she felt for him was lasting. This test would batter any relationship, let alone one as new and fragile as theirs.

"And if our feeling are of the lasting sort, then by damn I'm coming out of the closet!" Pen muttered, stacking the last of the pans in the dishwasher. She shut the lid with a snap of the locking mechanism, then washed her hands off of more than just dishes.

Libby was at another of her meetings, this time at the director of photography's rented house. With Pen in residence, Libby was keeping home meetings to a minimum—only those she was forced to have, such as the one she'd had over Mary Jane's costumes. Pen wondered if her cousin ever got a full night's sleep while on a movie project. From predawn preparation for the daily filming to late-night meetings that often went well past midnight, the pace was horrendous . . . and the results sometimes spectacular. Libby's last movie had been a touching one about star-crossed lovers. Critics had called it simplistic, but moviegoers had come out in droves. Libby found the common denominator of people's emotions. This was her cousin's biggest project yet, and she deserved to have it be successful.

Tired of reading, tired of watching TV, tired of everything, Pen wandered into the living room, touching a vase, a table, a lamp shade. She wanted desperately to go out, run around, scream in delight— experience anything but this cooped-up feeling. But she knew she'd stay in the house. Like a butterfly in a cocoon, she wasn't ready to emerge yet.

A pile of tapes on top of the VCR caught her eye, and she flipped through them, pausing at one in particular. Richard's first movie, the one in which he'd made his mark with a mass audience. She'd never seen the film, but now she was interested, very interested. She popped the tape into the machine and settled on the sofa.

The picture was good. Richard was *really* good. More than good, absolutely mesmerizing. He should have gotten an Academy Award, Pen thought. He was brilliant.

A scene began between Richard and the female lead, a woman partly innocent, partly temptress, an allegory for Eve, who was slowly pulling "Adam" down into the depths of evil. It was a love scene.

Pen watched the couple, her stomach tightening with each kiss. She knew what she'd seen on the set, but this looked so real. Anger rose within her, pure blind anger that made her sick, as clothes were shed and Richard and his costar were naked from the waist up. They began to . . .

When the scene cut away finally, Pen switched off the set and sat there in the growing darkness, unconscious of anything but the images inside her head. This was acting, a part of acting that many people felt enhanced a film. Not gratuitous or hard-core sex, but beautifully filmed lovemaking scenes that were integral to a movie. She and Richard had even had a conversation about it, but she hadn't been prepared for this. . . . How did husbands and wives of actors cope with this? Did they feel as she did, that they wanted to scream and tear up every copy of the film? She wanted to, and she had no right to the feeling.

She'd thought about this, considered it, but it had been so detached from her present that it seemed only a distant worry. But now she had been confronted with it first-hand. Would she be able to handle this?

She knew the answer instantly.

She couldn't.

NINE

Along with the disruption of reporters outside the home of Penelope Marsh, teacher at Warren Regional Elementary School, neighbors complained of a suspect creeping through the backyards. David and Michelle Fiarello also reported their dog was let loose from his chain, although he was recovered sometime later wandering on the south side of Blairstown, near the hunt club. Calls and inquiries to Ms. Marsh were not returned as of press time.

Richard set down the local weekly paper that had been innocently delivered to every mailbox in the county, including his, and wondered what disaster could happen next. The notion was mind-boggling, because he couldn't think how things could get worse. Here they were feeling all nice and safe from the big, bad tabloids, and the little tiny local rag up and pulls the scoop of the year—even if they didn't know it. Although the article simply mentioned the reporters at Pen's house, that would probably more than damning as far as her school board was be concerned.

Pen must be frantic, and that meant she'd be ready to drop him. He had to see her, reason with her. If she could reason. At least he had to try.

He went to Libby's house a few hours later under cover of night.

Pen practically yanked him off his feet and through the kitchen doorway, demanding, "What are you doing here?"

"Is that any way to greet a sister soul-mate?" he complained. Lolita rubbed her way against his calves, meowing happily. At least someone was glad to see him. He handed over the package he'd thought to bring, saying, "Here's the dress back. It's ripped under both arms. I think it was a size too small."

Tears were already welling in Pen's eyes, and he knew his lame joke had been in poor taste. He could only guess that she probably hated him for all the trouble he'd caused her. He stood frozen for a moment, not knowing what to do, this whole situation being beyond his ken. But she looked as if she needed to be held, and every instinct in his body was crying out for him to hold her. So he took a chance and stepped forward and put his arms around her.

"I'm sorry," he whispered, grateful that she didn't push him away. She didn't wrap her arms around him, but her fingers clutched his shirtfront. He rubbed her back, the gesture strictly a comforting one, although his veins caught a little swirl of heat.

She sniffed back more unshed tears. She didn't cry, not Pen. "Oh, hell, Richard. It's not your fault. And it's not mine."

"They can't do anything, Pen. You've conducted yourself with more moral concern for the kids than half that damn school board probably does." He set his jaw. "If there are repercussions, I'll come and testify."

"Oh, brother, that'll be a three-ring circus."

Libby's acid comment landed with its usual bang. Richard turned to face her, but didn't let go of Pen. He'd be damned before he'd do that anymore.

"You're here, Richard, screwing up again, after I told you not to," Libby went on.

"I needed to see Pen."

"And I needed to see him," Pen said stoutly, straightening out of his embrace. "It's okay, Libby."

Libby eyed them both for a long moment. "You are out the door by one, mister, and no argument. I don't have that many dresses to lend to you." She took the package from Pen and pulled out her dress. "Geez, I must be built like a linebacker if Richard could get into this one."

"I split the sleeves," Richard said helpfully.

"That makes me feel a whole lot better." Libby waved her hands. "Shoo! Upstairs before I change my mind. And, remember, out by one!"

"Yes, ma'am." Richard took Pen's hand and raced with her up the stairs.

"I should hate you," Pen said when she closed her bedroom door behind them.

He turned to face her, his heart thudding. "Do you?"

"No." It was a whisper, but it was enough. She smiled. "What a mess."

He took her back in his arms again. This time she came more willingly, wrapping her arms around his waist. Relief rolled over him, far more than he'd expected, telling him that not only had he needed her comfort and forgiveness more than he'd thought, but that he'd been more worried than he'd realized that he wouldn't get it.

"Don't apologize," she said.

"I wasn't going to." But he smiled, knowing he probably would have been apologetic in tone, if nothing else. She was getting to know him so well.

She started to laugh. "All this time I've been in hibernation over those stupid tabloids and the bomb's been in my own backyard."

"Brutus's actually," Richard said.

"True." She sighed. "I wish I didn't like my job as much as I do. It'll be hard to get another one as good."

"Bull." He grinned as she looked up at him in surprise. "Come to L.A., and they'll hire someone with your credentials in a second. And nobody will care if you're the current hottest item in the tabloids."

"You're the current hottest item, Richard. I'm just a by-product."

She drew in a deep breath. He could feel her breasts pressing into his chest, overturning his feelings of comfort. Desire blazed in him. He shuddered with restraint. He'd issued his invitation lightly, unconsciously really, but he knew it had been a testing of the waters. Suddenly he realized he didn't want to hear what she had to say.

Instead of drawing away, she tightened her arms around him and said, "I . . . I don't know if you meant the invitation seriously, but I don't think I can go to Los Angeles, Richard. My home is here."

"I see." He did see . . . and he envied her. He'd been happy halfway up the mountainside in his trailer, his inner self content. The mindset on the East Coast was different from that of the West, and he was more comfortable with it. In fact, his time here had only emphasized that his vagabond life was unsatisfying in too many ways. He needed and wanted home, hearth . . . and Pen. "It was just a suggestion. But there are things we can do here to help you. I know someone I can talk to. And I won't make things worse. I promise."

"I don't know . . ." She stepped out of the embrace, then sighed. "Dammit! Where's my spine? I'm tired of being cooped up here like I'm Hester Prynne with a big scarlet letter on my chest! Since the cat's half out of the bag, I'm damned if I'm hibernating any longer."

He grinned at her new spunk, but only said, "What about those tabloids? They'll be all over you."

"Let 'em," Pen snapped, folding her arms across her chest. "I'll borrow Brutus for a few weeks. I'm taking back my life, Richard. I'm damned anyway now, so I might as well. Besides, I've had enough of this nonsense."

"Is there any room for me?" he asked, his stomach tightening with fear that she might give him a negative answer.

She hesitated, and he knew immediately that she wanted to say no. She closed her eyes, shuddered, then opened them, saying, "Yes, for as long as you want to be there. I know I shouldn't, but . . . I want you. I care about you, Richard."

He drew her to him. "I won't hurt you, Pen. I promise."

She turned her head to look at him, her lips already moving to say something. He kissed her into silence, not wanting to hear any words.

The kiss turned heated, then desperate as they both tried to express with their bodies what was in their hearts. Words meant nothing against the longing and the need that could only be answered by the other.

This, Richard knew beyond any doubt, was what turned the ugly duckling into the graceful swan.

Somehow, despite all their obstacles, he would make it all work.

He was gone by one in the morning, true to his word—and with Libby pounding on the door to remind him. After a quick look outside, Richard went down the front steps, the quiet, deserted street giving him confidence. He whistled as he got into his Bronco, parked around the corner. Tomorrow he'd talk with Libby and the producers. A donation of film equipment to the school might smooth Pen's way later, especially if certain provisos were included.

He could feel all the future hurts hedging in, but the most important thing was that she wanted him now and in the immediate future. If she was ready to bull her way through this, then so was he, dammit.

He was coming out of the gate running.

Someone had been lucky with his camera. Very lucky.

Pen stared at the tabloid headlines as she stood in the supermarket checkout line. A picture of Richard, hazy but identifiable, covered three columns on the front page along with the headline: SEXY NEW STAR'S SHOCKING LOVE REVEALED. SHE'S HIS DIRECTOR!

Pen grabbed the paper and flipped through the pages until she found the article.

Despite recent rumors, things are more than hunky-dory on the set of the Richard Creighton movie. How could it not be when his new love is the film's director, Libby Marsh? Pictured coming out of her house after a late night tête-à-tête, Creighton refused to comment. The studio expects big things from this picture—and they're sure to get it now! Will Richard and Libby team up for wedding bells? Keep reading.

Several more pictures of Richard leaving Libby's house accompanied the text, which went on with background from Richard's and Libby's love lives. There wasn't much in Richard's case, a notion that oddly pleased Pen. She had no idea how they got a picture of Richard leaving Libby's. It boggled the mind how they got such information and were able to publish so quickly. The tabloid must have dropped everything to get it in after little more than three days.

"Hey, lady, are you reading or buying?"

Pen smacked the pages shut and dropped the offensive rag onto her groceries. "Buying."

The checker ran the bar code across the LED display. "Yeah, everybody is, with them making that film just up the road."

Pen couldn't get out of the store fast enough. She sat in the cars. Richard and Libby! Blared all across the nation's newsstands! Pen didn't know whether to laugh or cry and settled for doing both.

She made it home in record time. Not a single reporter graced her sidewalk. In fact, the street was deserted. It had been like this when she'd come home from Libby's. Now she knew why. Word must have gotten out immediately, and she'd been dropped like a hot potato in favor of the real news.

She felt half disappointed, then reminded herself not to be stupid.

Inside, Lolita greeted her enthusiastically. After setting down the groceries, Pen patted her cat absently, the blinking answering machine catching her eye. She counted the flashes, the total indicating how many calls she'd received.

Thirteen. Pen swallowed back a lump of anxiety. She didn't want to know, then hated herself for reaching out and gingerly pressing the Messages button.

The first call was from a neighbor, who was chuckling about having thought it was she who was involved with Richard, not her cousin Libby. The second call was the same. And the third. Right down the line, each call resembled the last with amused, apologetic friends, neighbors, and coworkers who wanted her to know the laugh was on them. Even the call from one of the school board members, amused and overly apologetic, didn't make her feel better.

"Ha, ha," she snapped when the calls were done. "Guess what you don't know."

She smacked the Erase button, then wondered what she was so angry about. Wasn't this what she wanted? Her normal life back? She ought to be grateful for the mistake. Now she could put things in order. Still, Libby! Who in her right mind would believe Richard was hot for Libby?

And he better not be.

"This is ridiculous," she muttered, slamming groceries away.

She had meant to break off with Richard, after seeing that love scene in his old movie. But when the little weekly paper had come out with its bomb, he had come to her, concerned and worried. And when she had looked into his eyes, she had seen the underlying fear of being rejected by her, being hurt. She hadn't been able to do it. Not for herself or for him. She wasn't ready to cut out her heart yet. She might never be.

But she couldn't live with seeing him in love scenes with other women. It took a more mature person than she was. She'd known from the beginning that she would be with him only for as long as the filming lasted in Blairstown. Now it was written in stone.

She brushed at the tears suddenly welling in her eyes. The phone rang. Another neighbor in the throes of amusement, she thought, picking it up.

"Yes, it's hysterical that everyone thought it was me," she said, without waiting for the voice. "Yes, my cousin has the hots for Richard Creighton, and, no, I don't have any juicy stories about them."

"I take it you've seen the latest tabloid," Richard said.

"No, I'm living on a mountaintop in Tibet," she replied, not able to keep the sarcasm from her voice. Determined to control herself, she said more calmly, "Yes, I've seen it."

"The whole thing is ludicrous," he said. "We need to talk."

"Richard . . ."

"Pen, please. I can't come to you."

She hadn't seen him since she'd come home, one restriction that was still on, for both their sakes. She closed her eyes, feeling the pull toward the inevitable well of doom.

"Pen."

"Yes. I'll come."

She put the receiver down, and a moment later it rang again. Sighing, she picked it up.

It was Libby. Laughing. "So how about this? I'm Richard's new love life. Is this a riot or what? All these clowns are camped on my doorstep now. I can't even go outside without umpteen microphones being shoved in my face! Naturally, I'm getting off great sound bites about the film. I'll have to thank my neighbor across the street. We found out he was the culprit with the camera who shot Richard that night. The producers weren't that thrilled at first, though. They were afraid it would ruin my control on the set, but they love the publicity now. Mary Jane's been a real bitch, though—"

"Libby," Pen said in warning.

The line went quiet. Finally her cousin said, "I guess you're not thrilled with this, either."

"No kidding. My ice cream is melting while I've been on the phone," Pen said, eyeing her still-packed groceries.

"So put the damn ice cream away. It's fattening anyway."

"Gee, thanks." But she moved toward her freezer, stretching out the cord on the wall phone in the process.

"Pen, I'm sorry this happened." Her cousin's voice was suddenly small and unsure, a miracle for Libby.

Pen sighed. "I know. Why do I feel like I'm caught up in a Marx Brothers movie without a script." She realized it was fairly early in the afternoon. "Where are you calling from? The set? Are you on a portable?" Her stomach tightened. "Didn't you tell me to stay off those things because people can listen in?"

"I'm home." Libby chuckled. "Barely got through the mob outside, which'll serve that neighbor right. The street's jam-packed. Mary Jane threw a fit and walked off the set, so filming had to be suspended."

"Oh, Good Lord!" Pen exclaimed. No wonder Richard wanted to see her.

"I'm letting her stew for a while before I go over and smooth her ruffled feathers—not that buzzards have that many."

Pen laughed.

"Richard's upset," Libby went on. "He needs you, Pen."

"He called." Pen closed her eyes. "I'm going to talk to him."

"Good. Pen, he's changed since he's been with you. It's been like watching a butterfly emerge. He's been good with the crew and patient with delays and problems. People really like him. And his performance is fabulous. But now he's withdrawing again. I'm worried about him. You need to come back on the set."

"You're only worried you won't get a good performance out of him now," Pen countered.

"Yes, his performance is being affected, but I'm his friend first. I was a tormentor once. I *know* what he went through as a kid. I'm truly worried for him personally. I'm not a complete monster, you know."

She tried another excuse. "But you said the tension was good for actors."

"Yes, but it's gotten ugly lately. You're so good for him, Pen. You need to be there." Her voice lightened. "I can hire you as a consultant."

"Nepotism," Pen told her.

"Hell, this is Hollywood. Nobody cares. Consider coming to the set."

"I told you, I'm not going to be ammunition for Mary Jane."

"You might be a cannon bomb that goes off in her face." Libby chuckled. "Consider that."

Later, as Pen drove to Richard's, she felt herself wavering on the subject of attending the shooting. Granted, the problem of her love life being revealed was gone, but she knew the real danger now was with the female costar. One meeting had told her that. No way would she put herself and Richard through what Mary Jane might do. The woman was to be avoided like the plague. Richard might need someone he could trust on the set, but he didn't need the complications her presence might entail. No, it was better this way.

No one had yet discovered his new home—clearly a very well kept secret still, so Pen turned down the dirt road. She had a feeling that even if a mass of reporters were present, they'd think she was a messenger between him and Libby.

Ironic.

Richard came out even before she stopped the car. She no sooner emerged from the vehicle than he had her in his arms, his mouth hot and desperate on hers in a devastating kiss.

"Richard," she murmured, breathless when he finally lifted his head.

"Damn, but I can't stand this," he muttered, burying his face in the curve of her neck. "I've missed you. I want us to be together. Again."

She wondered, for all his physical charisma and power, if the little hurt, lonely boy still didn't dwell close to the surface at times. A part of him *was* hurting; she could feel it.

She laughed, shakily. "I wonder what the tabloids would do with this picture?"

Richard chuckled. "Probably suppress it. Libby's a better story." He pulled away and looked at her. "Are you upset about this Libby thing?"

She rolled her eyes. "What a notion. But I think I'm grateful for it. She gets me off the hook, and she's eating this up. How are you? Are they bombarding you? I see they haven't found this place yet."

Richard snorted. "Saint Peter couldn't find this place. They aren't bugging me any more than they used to at the set. Which is to say nearly constantly. But I'm used to it. Pen, you know who I care about. You."

She grinned. "I know."

He kissed her again. "Let's go into the house."

Inside was still as sterile as she remembered it. No wonder Richard was becoming withdrawn again.

"I heard Mary Jane walked off the set today."

Richard uttered a curse she hadn't thought he'd even know. "You've been hanging around Libby too much."

"I've got a lot more of them too." He made a face. "I hate actors. What spoiled brats they are. She blew up because *I* missed my cue. Once."

"You're kidding."

He shook his head. "No. And I didn't miss my cue. But she threw a tantrum in front of everyone."

"I'm surprised you didn't strangle her," Pen said.

"Me too. But it had nothing to do with my missing cues. Mary Jane walked only because there's all this publicity and none of it's going in her direction. The producers will have a fit and blame me." He made another face. "I sound like I'm whining."

"No. Just mad."

"Hell, this is no way to make a picture, Pen. I can't stand to be on the set. There's nothing." He gazed at her. "This is a plum part for me. A great character, so well-rounded. Sweet Jesus, but you could see him leaping off the pages of the script. I can't look at the dailies; a lot of actors can't watch themselves. But I feel it. Or I did before Mary Jane got to the set. And Libby's doing a helluva job. She's going to get an Academy Award nomination—if one prima donna doesn't take the whole thing down."

"It's really bad, isn't it?"

"You have no idea how bad."

Words were left unsaid, but they hovered in the air. Tangible. Waiting.

Pen sighed, knowing she had to face facts and her responsibility to two people she loved. "I suppose since Libby is now your true love in the eyes of the media, I could come up to the set. Or maybe you don't want me to."

He pulled her to him and practically growled, "You know damn well I do. I need a friend, Penelope Marsh."

With a lazy, promising smile, she rocked herself intimately against him. "A friend like this?"

"You bet." His arms tightened around her. "And one I can trust too."

His mouth came down on hers.

Pen drove onto the set, her stomach tight with knots even before she spotted the mob of reporters being held behind a barrier by several security men who looked as if they meant business. She parked the car behind several perimeter trailers and got out to brave the gauntlet.

Her nerves danced as several looked curiously at her. If they knew who she was, they didn't show any interest. Neither was any interest shown when she murmured her name to the one security guard with a clipboard. She was checked off and let through. A round of groans went up from behind her, but only because she'd been admitted and the stringers hadn't.

An odd disappointment rose inside her, and she grinned, knowing she was being idiotic to be miffed that she was a nobody again. Even if she boldly announced she and not Libby was Richard's "item," she was positive they'd think she was lying to protect her cousin.

But as she emerged into the area of actual filming, another kind of anxiety took over.

She was definitely back in the lion's den.

TEN

Richard spotted Pen as she slowly approached the edges of the filming area. She looked as if she were being forced to walk the plank, he thought, but it felt so damn good to see her. More than good. He wanted to run over and drag her into his arms, then kiss her senseless. He knew he couldn't, but he felt ready for anything now—including another of Mary Jane's temper tantrums.

The crew and those cast members who knew Pen greeted her cheerfully and with genuine smiles. It had been a while since anyone had seen those, he thought as he made his way toward her.

"Old George the Third in the midst of Washington's army wouldn't look as glum as you, miss," he said, stopping short and not touching her. But he drank her in with his gaze, the light flowery skirt and long sleeveless vest hiding nothing of the body he knew as well as his own. Her sandals were a couple of straps and no more. Although he had no interest in toes, he had to admit that the effect of the delicate sandals was sensual. "Or as pretty."

"Everything looks quiet on the frontier, Mr. Freemont," she commented, smiling as she shaded her eyes against the brutal August sun while glancing around the set.

"Quiet now that reinforcements have arrived—and you're a damn sight better lookin' than these folks." She was keeping him in character. He needed it. He'd felt as if he'd lost the thread of Ezekiel with Mary Jane's disruptions.

She grinned. "What *do* you wear under that loincloth, anyway?"

"Just you whenever possible."

Her face colored and he chuckled. Maybe Ezekiel was wearing off on him. They kept their voices low so no one would overhear. Richard knew it looked as if he were only exchanging pleasantries with the cousin of his latest "woman." The urge to laugh nearly overwhelmed him, but he pushed it away. The urge to kiss her was more troublesome to control.

"Mary Jane hasn't graced us with her presence yet," he continued, deciding that if the discussion kept up in the same vein, he would be "up" before long. "She's three hours late. Every TV show from 'Entertainment Tonight' to Joan Rivers's gossip segment has picked up on the tabloids, so I wonder if she'll even appear. I wish I could touch you."

"Better not." But the words never reached her eyes. In them were reflected the desire of all the nights they'd shared. "Libby looks calm, considering her female star is late."

Richard glanced over at Pen's cousin, who was watching the playback camera which showed a continuously running videotape they made of the production. "She does, doesn't she? All I know is that she says Mary Jane is fine now and she'll be here."

"You're calm too."

"Because you're here."

"And sassy."

"Because you're here." He lifted his hair from his neck, the August heat getting to him, and pulled a rubber band from his leather ammunition bag to wrap his hair in a tail while they were waiting. The linen shirt was cool enough, but the leggings and mocs didn't breathe. Everyone was wilting while they waited on the "star."

Finally a murmur of relief began at one end of the set, slowly growing as people parted. Richard turned with Pen to see Mary Jane striding through the crowd. She was dressed in street clothes, clearly not even close to being ready to film. He felt Pen stiffen beside him and glanced at her in puzzlement. He opened his mouth to ask what was wrong when Mary Jane checked her gait in front of him.

"You look terrible, Richard," she said, eyeing him. "Like you're ready to collapse."

"You're not looking so cool yourself," he told her in return, not allowing her an inch in the war she'd chosen to wage. It was obvious that whatever Libby had done to get her back on the set, she hadn't managed to change the lady's attitude. He added, "I guess we both better visit makeup ASAP."

Someone had the nerve to twitter in the ensuing silence. A murderous look came into Mary Jane's eyes. Richard merely smiled innocently at her.

"You're the little cousin, aren't you?" Mary Jane said to Pen, clearly deciding she was the next victim.

"That's me," Pen replied in a cheerful voice that made Richard wonder if he'd imagined her earlier tension. "*Little* . . . and Libby's cousin."

Mary Jane smiled maliciously. "You haven't been around for a while. Where've you been?"

"Vacation."

"Well, you've really missed some hot stuff with Libby and Richard here. I'm surprised their *affair* didn't get out sooner."

Richard immediately opened his mouth to deny Mary Jane's words when Pen laughed. It was an easy one, filled with good humor. "If you think they're bad here, you should see them at home."

Richard decided Ezekiel would grin and keep his tail out of the cat fight, so he just grinned and kept his tail out of the cat fight.

"Mary Jane, my angel!" Libby called out, coming over to them. "You're here. Go get into costume in your nice cool trailer. We have a sweet little flirtation scene, where you shine. Pen, be a love and babysit my darling Richard while we're waiting. I have several things to go over with the lighting people, and you're the only one I can trust with this sexy hunk. I wouldn't want him overheating, either. You can use his trailer."

Libby patted Richard on the cheek—not the one on his face. He hoped he didn't flinch in surprise.

Mary Jane's expression was positively ugly, and he expected her to walk straight off the set again. But she whipped around and headed for her trailer. The wardrobe girl raced after her. The entire set breathed a collective sigh of relief.

"I'm surprised she didn't hit you," Pen murmured to her cousin.

"Control." The two of them laughed.

As they walked to his trailer Richard said, "Want to tell me what that 'control' bit with Libby meant?"

"A joke between cousins." Pen eyed him. "What *have* you and Libby been doing while I was in hibernation?"

"Being wild and passionate," he said with a straight face. "Don't you read the papers? Can I kill Mary Jane and get away with it?"

"You'll have to wait in line . . . behind me."

As soon as they were inside his trailer, he backed

her against the door, plastered himself against her, and kissed her thoroughly. Cool air wafted over his skin but didn't chill the heat building inside him.

"I'm not sure this is the babysitting Libby had in mind," Pen said breathlessly as he spread kisses along her shoulder.

"It is. Trust me." He kissed her again on the lips.

"This is dangerous." But Pen's hands were trailing down his back, her fingers kneading his flesh through the light shirt.

"Not this," he muttered as his blood surged dangerously. "Making love to you is as necessary as breathing and eating. Meet me at the house tonight. I need you."

"I need you."

Things hadn't progressed to the necessities of life when the call came to return to the set, but Richard took his mark near the fort's wall in exactly the right frame of mind for a flirtation scene. Easy and relaxed . . .

"And . . . action," Libby called.

"Line," Mary Jane immediately requested, blowing the entire mood.

Richard waited patiently as Mary Jane was fed her line. He glanced at Pen, resisting the urge to exchange an intimate smile. Somehow her presence gave him the patience to abide the nonsense. When Mary Jane was ready again, Libby called for action.

They got a three-sentence exchange filmed when Mary Jane announced, "Richard's off. I can't get into it."

"Sorry," Richard said, deciding not to argue the point. It wasn't worth it, and it would only hold everything up.

They tried the scene again.

"The sun's in my eyes," Mary Jane suddenly complained. "I can feel myself squinting."

"Kill the sun!" Libby called out as everyone groaned and began running to reposition equipment.

Mary Jane smiled smugly at Richard. "By the way, I've got a big interview with 'Entertainment Tonight.' It'll be their lead. Isn't that terrific? It's about time *someone* talked about the film."

"Great," Richard said, feeling the stab. He knew this was what had lured the woman back. And she was throwing it out to him to upset his emotional balance yet again. He refused to permit it. "You'll do a good job, I'm sure. I turned them down three times last month, so the publicist will be happy they went for someone else."

Mary Jane stiffened. Richard knew it was petty, but her manipulations grated on his nerves. If this scene even approached quality, it would take a helluva acting job on his part.

The scene began once again. This time it was Libby who called a halt to the proceedings. Richard glared at his director, wondering what was wrong now. Mary Jane was finally cooperating, having run out of complaints.

"Mary Jane's a little too much in the shade now, and we can't see her face. Set the light reflectors back a little, and we'll try it again."

They tried it again. Libby yelled "Cut" about halfway through the scene. And she did it once more—without even looking up from the clipboard on her lap. In neither case did she say what the problem was.

"What?!" Mary Jane screamed in frustration. "What's wrong now?"

"I'm not really sure," Libby mused, her gaze going back to the clipboard. "Try it again."

Richard set his jaw, the retakes beginning to get on his nerves, too, when he noticed Libby exchange a swift look with Pen. That "control" talk earlier suddenly fell into place. Libby was controlling her actors, not the other way around. The whole bit, from playing along with the tabloids to asking for retake after retake without explaining why, was designed to put Mary Jane in her place. Subtle, but clearly effective.

Richard relaxed, willing to reshoot the scene for the next ten years. He decided the producers ought to pay Pen just for showing up.

She was definitely good for the picture—and positively essential for him.

"Okay!" Libby called out. "That's a wrap for today. Remember, everyone, on Monday we move into the New York set for the big love scene. Buses leave Sunday afternoon from the college for those of the crew who are needed."

Pen tensed at her cousin's last words. What big love scene? Richard had never said anything before about a *big* love scene. Neither had Libby.

"That ought to be some acting," a crew member said to another as they passed by her. Others around her were already talking about the prospects of going into the city for a few days. A few days! How the hell long did a love scene take to film?

Maybe it was between Mary Jane and her character's husband, she told herself, even though she had a sinking feeling it wasn't. Watching the flirtation scene was enough. Not really flirtation, more like tentative admissions of their feelings for each other. Even with the disruptions, it had been almost painful to watch Richard gaze at another woman the way he had. But a full love scene . . . a few days . . . his dislike of Mary Jane could turn to something else entirely.

She couldn't even stand the thought. It was her worst nightmare come true.

Libby walked over to her. "It was great to have you here today." Her voice lowered. "Really good for you-know-who. How did I do with my crabby child?"

Pen couldn't help smiling. "You were a bitch in control. I don't think anyone but her minded."

"It was time to let her know things would be different." Libby grinned.

Pen refused to ask, didn't want to ask, wasn't going to ask . . . "What's this about a love scene?"

"The biggie in the movie between Charlotte and Ezekiel." Libby shrugged. "It's no big deal."

"You just said it was a biggie. Is it . . ." Pen swallowed back the bile rising in her throat. "Is it a nude scene?"

Somebody called Libby away before she could answer. She patted Pen's shoulder. "Don't worry about it."

"Don't worry about it," Pen muttered under her breath, heading for her car. She passed the line of reporters without even breaking her stride and got in her car. Again none of them showed any interest in her, so her visit to Richard's trailer had been accepted at face value—if they'd even heard about it. Not that she was worried about that now.

She was pulling into her driveway when she remembered Richard had asked her to meet him at his house after the day's shooting. She pushed the gearshift into "park" and just sat there with the motor running, knowing the last place she wanted to go was Richard's. He'd never said a word about this upcoming love scene.

"You're a coward, Pen Marsh," she said. "Yeah, I know."

She jammed the gear back in "drive" and peeled out of her driveway. Richard wasn't there yet when she arrived. She didn't wonder why she was there waiting, against all her good judgment. She knew.

She was in love. And she hated it.

Despite all the impossible obstacles, she'd fallen in love. And like a doormat, she kept coming back for more. Because she knew there wouldn't be much more, she acknowledged. Because she didn't care about the heartbreaking aftermath; she wanted desperately what was the "now." It was a bargain she'd made from the beginning with herself. And it was one she needed to keep.

Richard finally arrived in an electrical supply truck from the set. He got out of the cab after a comment to the security man behind the wheel.

The moment the truck was out of view on the private road, Richard swept her up into his kiss. Pen forgot everything as she lost herself in sheer sensation. Nothing mattered when he kissed her like this. And he always kissed her like this, as if she were the most important woman in the world and he couldn't get enough of her.

"Richard," she murmured, clinging to him helplessly when he finally eased his mouth away.

He just laughed. "See what having you on the set does to me?"

They went inside the house, Pen not quite sure how she walked on her wobbly legs to get there.

"Will you come to New York with me?" Richard asked as he dropped his backpack on a foyer chair.

Pen blinked, nowhere near ready to deal with the question, let alone the problem. "Uh . . . I wanted to talk to you about that."

He turned around, something in her tone having given away her apprehension. "You will go, won't you? I've been planning to surprise you with it tonight, but Libby spoiled it with her announcement. Pen, we'll have a few days together out of Blairstown and in anonymous New York. I'm in a suite at the Plaza Hotel."

"But . . ." she began, struggling to find the right words that wouldn't make her vulnerable.

"If you're worried about people finding out, don't." He laughed. "All the rooms were taken in the producer's name, and the hotel's reputation for being discreet is above reproach. They wouldn't survive if they weren't. Besides, nobody's going to budge from the notion that Libby and I are a hot item."

She nodded, then looked away. "The love scene . . ."

"No big deal," he said, shrugging. "I'll gag my way through it."

Pen closed her eyes against the sick feeling inside her. She didn't want to go. She couldn't go.

"Are you jealous?"

Pen opened her eyes to find Richard turned back around and grinning at her. She cleared her throat.

"Well . . . uh, no. I just wondered if it would be a . . . a nude one."

"I love it," he said, pulling her into his embrace. "No, it won't be a nude one. But you don't have to go the studio if you don't want. Just come with me to the hotel. It'll be private and we'll have some free time together."

"I told you I couldn't handle it," she muttered, disgusted with giving so much of her emotions away.

"Then you better come to the hotel and make sure I'm a good boy," he murmured, nuzzling her ear. He ran his tongue around it, sending shivers of sensuality down her spine. Then he teased her lobe with his teeth.

Pen moaned and arched herself against him.

She couldn't not go, she thought dimly. She couldn't not go.

The suite was luxurious and private and sensual. Everything he'd thought it would be.

Pen stood by the sitting room's floor-to-ceiling windows, looking out over Central Park.

"This beats the hell out of my trailer, doesn't it?" he asked, coming up next to her to admire the view.

She raised her eyebrows. "Won't all this opulence ruin your frame of mind for your character?"

"Ezekiel can handle himself for a while. This is for

me. For us." He pulled her against his side, liking the sound of "us."

Pen clearly liked it, too, for she put her arms around his waist and rested her head on his chest. He hadn't realized just how much she'd come to mean to him. He opened his mouth to say so, when some inner voice cautioned him. They were still fragile together, and he didn't want to rush her.

"Let's get unpacked," he said, "And order dinner in. I want this to be only for us."

Later that night, when she emerged from the bathroom in a lavender negligee, Richard decided he'd stumbled onto a wealth of great ideas.

The air froze in his lungs as he lay on the four-poster bed and surveyed the sheer lace bodice and panel that ran down the front of the gown. His script slipped down his side as he stared. Every intimate detail of her, from her rosy nipples to the soft down at the junction of her thighs, was veiled and completely exposed at the same time. Amazing what the contrary stimuli did to a man's pulse, he thought. His heart thumped painfully in his chest. And what it did to the rest of him was downright sinful. He was so tight, he was straining against his silk boxers.

She came toward him without a word, watching his expression with a slight smile of recognition. She knew exactly what she was doing to him. She took the script the rest of the way out of his lifeless hands and set it on the night table. But she didn't click off the lamp. Instead, she leaned across the bed, her hair falling forward against her breast, and brushed her lips against his. She didn't touch him anywhere else, just her lips rubbing and sucking at his own, coaxing his mouth open to a bolder kiss. Her tongue ran along his bottom lip, then inside to swirl along his own.

He drew in a deep, shuddering breath and reached for her. But she pushed his arms down, insistent on only their mouths touching in a slow, erotic kiss that exploded through the senses. Again and again, when he would have pulled her to him, she held him back, teaching him the finer points of slow, deep kisses that drove men insane. Richard realized he was perfectly willing to learn. Anytime, anywhere, anyplace.

Finally her mouth eased from his . . . but only to trail a light string of sensual fire along his jaw and down his chest. Her tongue ringed his nipple, nearly sending him shooting off the bed. Her fingers raked through the mat of hair on his chest, her nails gently stinging down the muscles of his stomach. He groaned and clenched his fist in the spread, wrapping the quilting around his hands in a Herculean effort not to touch her. She'd made it more than clear she was seducing him, and he'd be a fool to stop her in her quest. Of course, there was a definite possibility she'd kill him in the process.

Her fingers hooked around the waistband of the shorts and slowly slid them down his hips. The feel of the tight silk against the most intimate part of his body was sheer torture. His blood felt as if it had been heated in a furnace beyond the boiling point.

He wanted to say something, tell her what she was doing to him, but he couldn't seem to find his voice. With each touch of her mouth against his skin, she knew.

And then she straddled him, taking him inside of her. She smiled knowingly. "Now you're properly covered."

She moved against him. He gritted his teeth at the sensation of her caressing him tightly in her moist heat, the silken gown puddled around his stomach and thighs. She rose above him almost leisurely, stroking him again and again, her eyes closed, her head thrown back. He gripped her thighs, trying to anchor himself to her. Her movement quickened. Her hands curled against the hair arrowing his stomach, tiny little pinpoints of pleasure-pain.

Richard could stand it no longer. He cried out as his body exploded into a thousand blinding pieces. Pen moaned, arching impossibly against him, taking in all of him, everything he had. Everything he was.

She collapsed against his chest, quivering at the sensual shock waves rolling through them. He wrapped her in his embrace, touching her at last, in the aftermath of a cocooning velvet darkness.

She leaned up, gathering strength from a place he couldn't begin to fathom, and kissed him. "That was a *real* love scene, and don't you forget it."

He managed a chuckle. "Lady, it's burned in my memory forever."

"It better be." She caressed his chest, her finger-tips trailing across his skin like a cool wildfire.

Richard rubbed his hand lightly along her shoulder, delighting in the feel of her silken flesh that far surpassed the most expensive silk for evoking tactile sensations. She had given him more than she would ever know, for her to seduce him like that. She had been sexually bold before—they both had with each other—but never like this. He wanted it to go on forever.

He wanted forever to begin now.

She should have stayed away.

Pen swallowed back the queasy feeling in her gut as she watched the lighting crew put the finishing touches on the equipment hanging above a three-sided set that looked exactly like a diorama on settler life in a history museum. The life-size set itself was dwarfed by the enormous soundstage they were in. A man and woman, both remarkably the same heights and builds as the principal stars, stood in place for the crew's benefit.

Pen wished they were doing the damn scene and not Richard. She'd managed to blend into a darkened corner, out of everybody's way, but it wasn't enough to avoid seeing the upcoming scene.

She had told herself last night before she and Richard had made love, *after* she and Richard had made love, first thing this morning, and all through getting dressed that she wouldn't attend the day's filming. She'd tour New York. She'd sleep in. She'd sit in the hotel lobby. She'd go get mugged in Central Park. Anything was preferable to watching this.

And yet she couldn't stay away. Now it was too late.

Pen rubbed her fingers across her forehead, trying to dispel the pounding behind her eyes. She'd have a migraine, she was sure, even though she'd never had one in her life before. There was always a first time, and this was certainly the event that would do it.

People were gathered around the small buffet table, digging into the pastries and coffees, but the conversations were low and somber. Richard and Mary Jane were both at the double-back makeup mirror, being done up. They didn't speak, but that didn't reassure her. Mary Jane's artfully tousled hair and small pert body were an allure few men could ignore. Pen felt too tall, too Alfred E. Neuman in coloring, and too gauche. The woman's presence made a mockery out of Pen's silly attempt at seduction the night before. She groaned in shame. Richard might have enjoyed it, but he had to be secretly amused by the whole thing.

"There you are," Libby said, peering at her as she walked over. "What are you doing over here?"

"Staying out of the way." Pen forced herself to smile.

Libby wasn't fooled. "Will you relax! This is no big deal. Oh, it'll look erotic as hell on the screen. But that's because of camera angles and all."

"Then why is the set closed?" Pen asked, raising her eyebrows.

"Because I don't need any nonsense distractions around. Besides, it's not closed. It's just not open. We have a bunch of damn reporters outside again. How the hell they found us, I don't know."

"Here you are," Richard said, coming up behind Libby.

"So much for this being an out-of-the-way corner," Pen muttered. "Judge Crater would have been found ages ago if you two had been on the trail."

Richard frowned. "What's wrong?"

He was in full colonial regalia, the scene being that his character would come looking for Robertson and instead would find the wife alone. They would consummate their forbidden love just one time. The damn scene had all the potential for gut-wrenching sexuality, Pen thought, having peeked at the script when Richard had been in the shower that morning.

"She's got a case of observer nerves," Libby replied for her cousin. She patted Pen's hand, then added. "Five minutes, Richard."

"I shouldn't have come," Pen said, sighing, after Libby left them alone.

"Yes, you should." Richard turned around and called out. "Set up my chair for Ms. Marsh."

"Richard, please!" Pen exclaimed in horror. "I don't want to be over there by the set."

"But how will I see you for inspiration?" he asked reasonably as he drew her out of her haven of dark safety.

"I doubt I'll be inspiring," she muttered, disgusted with her weaknesses. If only she'd stayed at the hotel . . . if only she'd stayed home altogether. Now she was forced to watch the man she loved make love to another woman. Once had been more than enough, and that had been "scenus interruptus" by a war party of Chickasaw Indians. That wouldn't happen this time.

She died inside as Richard placed the chair where he felt he'd have full view, then helped her into it, his gestures solicitous.

"Places, everyone," the assistant director called out.

Richard didn't move. Instead, he stared at her as he took her hands. Her heart began to beat faster, her senses suddenly attuned to his. But the vague anticipation did not prepare her for what came next.

"I love you, Pen. God, how I love you," he said, then kissed her lingeringly, his lips emphasizing his words.

When he finally released her, she stared at him in astonishment. Richard, the shy, private man, had exposed his emotions for all to see, for her to know and to make no mistake that whatever was required of the movie was only acting, a far, far cry from what he felt for her.

She wanted to say words, but her brain and her voice seemed to have been lifted straight out of her body. He grinned crookedly at her, kissed her again, then released her hands and strode onto the set, taking up his mark with Mary Jane. Dimly, somewhere in the recesses of her head, she was aware of the stares of the crew.

"And . . . action!" Libby called out, into the stunning silence.

Pen watched the scene begin, watched take after take for choreographing, watched the actors play their parts to the hilt. But mostly she watched Richard, watched each time he immediately turned to her at each disruption, watched him gaze at her in those moments, watched him smile intimately at her, only for her, and knew that he did love her, with every unspoken caress more powerful than what the camera would ever see.

And she said back to him with every look, every gesture, every smile, "I love you." The barriers were down and stripped away forever, leaving her heart bared to him. To everyone. It didn't matter anymore. Nothing mattered, except Richard and how much she loved him.

At the first full break, she rose up to meet Richard as he crossed the soundstage to her. His shirt was hanging open from the last bit of staging, and she grabbed up a handful, pulling him against her.

"You certainly know how to sweep a girl off her feet and leave her speechless," she murmured.

He grinned. "You taught one helluva lesson last night."

"And you taught one this morning. I love you, Richard."

"Damn straight you do." He kissed her soundly.

People chuckled at them, but Pen didn't care. The crew was loose and relaxed now, a far cry from the tenseness of the morning. When he finally let her go, Libby applauded, bringing more laughter from everybody. Pen found herself grinning at her cousin, who didn't look at all annoyed at her star's declaration. In fact, she looked damned pleased.

"Let's go get some lunch," Richard said, putting his arm around her. "I'm starved. But since we can't satisfy that, then let's eat."

Pen smiled at him. "You wait until tonight."

"Does that mean I'm going to get seduced again? I hope, I hope."

"If you're a very good boy," Pen promised.

The cameraman called Richard over at that moment, and Pen decided to move on outside, wanting to be alone with her thoughts. Her brain still reeled from his revelation.

As soon as she opened the stage door, however, she found herself standing behind a Mary Jane gleefully holding court with a mob of tabloid reporters. Belatedly she remembered Libby's words about the media showing up at the soundstage.

She grappled with the door latch, but Mary Jane yanked her forward, saying, "Here she is! Here's the *real* woman in Richard Creighton's life. Her cousin's been a hoax. Richard just told her in front of *everyone* that he loved her. Her! Not Libby Marsh. Her! The schoolteacher! They haven't been honest with your readers. And Richard certainly hasn't been honest with his fans."

As Pen gaped at the microphones suddenly shoved in her face, she also belatedly remembered how subdued Mary Jane had been during the filming. If she'd thought anything at all, it was that Libby had firm control finally. Certainly not that Mary Jane was furious and hatching plots. Her stomach clenched as questions were thrown at her.

"Is it true?"

"What about you two? How long have you been seeing each other?"

"Will you get married?"

"You and Richard *have* been dishonest with his fans. How do you answer that?"

"And how did you feel witnessing his love scene with Mary Jane?"

Mary Jane smiled at the questions prying beyond any definition of good sense and common courtesy, triumphant over the havoc she'd just wreaked.

Pen took a deep breath and raised her hands for quiet, staring each one of them in the eye while raising her eyebrows and simply waiting for quiet. The reporters obeyed remarkably fast, she decided, as the shouting died down. She knew she had to be very careful about what she said, because it could reflect poorly on Richard.

"Thank you." She smiled at them. "It's lovely to meet each of you today. Regarding the last question, I would like to say that today I have just been privileged to witness the greatest job of acting by anyone." Mary Jane gasped. Reporters twittered. Pen kept her face straight and continued innocently, "I'm so proud of Richard, of his entire performance in this movie. This is a beautiful love story and a terrific action adventure that certainly won't disappoint his fans, of which, I admit, I am one of his biggest." A second ripple of amusement spread through the group. "Richard and I have known each other for a long time, since we were children." She could feel Mary Jane start as well as see the reporters' surprise. Pen sensed no one would interrupt if they thought she'd give them information voluntarily. "It was never anyone's intent to be deceitful, only discreet. I have been very concerned for the children I work with. Their welfare and my school's reputation is very important to me. I'm sorry you all mistakenly got the wrong end of the story with my cousin, but I can't say I was displeased." More laughter. She grinned. "And I'm sure you understand.

Thank you for listening, but you'll have to excuse me now. I'm late for lunch."

"Wait! Wait!"

Pen only waved to them as she ducked back into the building again, leaving Mary Jane to fend for herself. Richard was right at the door. And he was grinning.

"I thought I was going to have to rescue you," he said, hugging her. "But you had them hopping through hoops."

"Thanks." Pen gripped his shirtfront and buried her face in his chest, feeling weak and drained from the experience.

She'd managed to hold her own today, but she'd never survive the attention his career drew all the time.

Never.

ELEVEN

"I'd like a word with you."

Pen stood in front of Mary Jane, blocking her from returning to the set after the lunch break. She'd sent Richard off to makeup and waited for his costar to come back into the building, having put two and two together and come up with a firm four. It was time to become the schoolteacher again. Besides, she couldn't be hurt any worse than Mary Jane had already managed, and she had had enough.

Mary Jane stared at her defiantly. "I don't want a word with *you*—"

"You'll have one," Pen broke in. "In my profession I'm well trained to recognize children who deliberately create negative attention for themselves and manipulate others. You're a classic case, Mary Jane. Textbook classic. It's obvious you've been the one who's been feeding the press erroneous information, hurtful information. It stops today."

"I don't know what you're talking about," Mary Jane said in regal tones.

"Yes, you do. I'm not playing games with you. I'm telling you to stop now. Libby's treated you well. And so has Richard. The rest of the cast and crew have endured your antics with patience. But you look foolish, Mary Jane. And obvious." A good teacher always gave her students an out so that they could regain their self-respect. It was time to give Mary Jane hers. Her tone softened. "You are a wonderful actress, Mary Jane. You can meet Richard as a respected colleague and give a performance he'll find tough to beat. Throwing someone off balance outside the arena of acting to undermine them only demeans you. You are far better than that. And in Richard's case it's not effective. As a child, he had to handle a lot worse abuse than you or anyone can deal out now. Be as secure as he is, Mary Jane. Take pride in yourself and your abilities. You have a right to it."

Mary Jane gaped at her.

Pen smiled. "Try it my way. You'll like the results much better."

She walked away, heading for her observer's chair so generously donated by Richard. He caught up with her halfway there.

"What was that all about?" he asked, putting his arm around her. "Giving her fair warning that she's dead before the day's out?"

"Just telling her what a wonderful actress she is." Pen chuckled, tucking her arm around his waist. It was nice to be open with him finally.

Richard raised his eyebrows. "I'll bet. I intend to have a talk with her myself. I believe she's the one who's been feeding the stringers all along and keeping them around."

Clearly he was as good at adding two and two as she was. Pen smiled, but shook her head. "Why bother? She only hurt herself, because they have *no* interest in her. Besides, you might see a change in her."

He made a face. "What on earth did you say to her?"

"What I told you: that she's a wonderful actress." Pen paused, then giggled. "Okay, so it's a long shot."

"You amaze me." But he seemed to let it go as the actors and crew were called for.

As the afternoon wore on, Pen's earlier concerns about dealing with the press on a continual basis were further complicated by talk among some of the crew that the filming would be wrapping up soon in New Jersey.

The next day the complications mounted even more when she discovered that her mail contained a memo from school on the times for the teachers to go in and prepare their classes for the fall. All of them combined only reminded her of the many barriers that were too high for her and Richard to scale—no matter how much they wanted to.

Her heart aching, she wondered how something so wonderful as a declaration of love could bring such despair.

Coming back to film a few more outdoor shots emphasized to Richard how much he would miss the East—miss his home state.

He chuckled to himself as he swiped at his sweaty forehead with the wide sleeve of his old-fashioned shirt. "Hot and humid" was an understatement for the weather, he thought. He defied Florida to come up with summers as brutal as some that New Jersey produced. And here he was missing it a breath ago.

"My God, how did the colonial women survive?" Mary Jane muttered, lifting the hem of her costume's long skirt and mopping her face with it. Then she cursed at smearing her makeup.

"They were tough women," Richard said, courteously lifting her hair off her nape to help cool down his costar while they stood on their marks and waited for the final adjustments to lights before the scene's filming began. The scene called for her hair to be loose, unfortunate on a blistering August day. He asked the nearest crew member to get Mary Jane some water.

"Thanks," she said, surprise clear in her voice.

"You're welcome." Richard shrugged. The woman had been positively pleasant over the last few days.

He had no idea what Pen had said to her, but it was working. Or maybe it hadn't been Pen at all. Maybe the way Mary Jane's impromptu press conference backfired made her subdued. Whatever, he had to admit she was finally giving one damn fine performance, one so good that Libby was muttering about refilming the earlier scenes.

Richard grinned as he thought of Pen meeting him later at the house. She was working in her classroom today. He missed her, but everything was going well. The press had cooled off and made her their darling. Her school board hadn't uttered a peep about him and her, which made him wonder if the studio's generous donation of film equipment had helped. And their relationship was out of the closet. They had a solid base to build from now. He felt as if he'd turned the corner on the Cretin forever. It was amazing what love with the right woman could do.

Tonight he had an important question to ask her. Very important.

But later at the house Richard felt all of his earlier thoughts crumbling to nothing as he gazed at the distress on Pen's face.

"What's wrong?" he asked immediately.

"Nothing." She shrugged in dismissal as she cut green pepper strips for salad.

"Was there a problem at the school today? Anyone give you a hard time about us?"

She shook her head. The pained expression subsided, but she was clearly forcing herself to be normal as she answered. "It went fine. But I'm tired. The heat was horrible at school. I dread setting up my classroom in it. All that getting up and down on ladders, moving desks, tables, and piles of books."

He listened to her babble on, knowing that was all she was doing in order to cover up whatever was troubling her.

"We're wrapping up the filming here in a few days," he said. "The rest of the interior shots will be done in New York and Los Angeles."

She nodded. "I see."

Something in her voice was odd, and he realized that he hadn't said anything about them, their future. Grinning at his stupidity, he said, "You'll come with me, of course. We'll be at the Plaza for the next few weeks, then we'll move on—"

"I'm not going."

Richard rounded on her, shocked. She stood frozen, not looking at him. "But why? Have I done something—"

"No." She shook her head vehemently, then raised her chin. "I live here, Richard. I work here. I love what I do. I can't give it up—"

He gripped her shoulders and spun her to face him, staring straight into her eyes. "Have I asked you to give anything up?"

"No." She glanced away, then back. "No, you haven't. Not yet. Richard, your job is not here, it's thousands of miles away. We both know who would have to give up a job, be flexible. We both know it's—"

"But why break things off now?" he demanded, dropping his hands as if touching her repulsed him. In a way, it did. She had no idea of the knife she was driving into his heart. "We can work out a solution, Pen. If we *try*, dammit! And you're not trying!"

"Because I know it won't work." She turned away. "If it's not the distance, it's going to be something else. Richard, the love scenes . . . I can't stand them. I can't handle the life you need to lead to be happy within yourself. And I won't make you change for me. Because I love you too much to do that."

"Then don't do this!" He pulled her back and kissed her, tasting her mouth, tasting her response to him. How could she talk one way and respond in another?

She eased out of his embrace, leaving him shaken. "I can't handle the love scenes. I can't handle the fishbowl."

"There's no fishbowl, dammit! And don't watch the love scenes. Lots of spouses don't watch them being filmed," he said, desperately trying to reason with her. "You know I love you. You know I'll come to you each time before a love scene and tell you that because *I* need to, not because I think I have to reassure you. I'll do it because you mean everything to me—"

"Richard, please." She stumbled away from him, out of the kitchen. "I . . . I can't."

"Pen!" He went after her.

She picked up her purse. "Richard, it's better this way."

Her voice was steady and her eyes were dry.

Richard tried to find the right words to keep her from doing this, but none came to mind. Of all the characters he'd played or seen, not one had the words to stop Pen from leaving him. Only he, Richard Creighton, was left. "Don't. Don't do this."

"I have to."

She was gone.

As he listened to the car's engine start up, as he listened to the spin of tires on the gravel, he knew her reasons had nothing to do with distance or even love scenes. He hadn't changed; he never would. He was the Cretin. Pen, who knew him from childhood, who knew the truth, couldn't stand knowing she'd be permanently entangled with him.

It was as simple as that.

"You what?"

Pen glared at her cousin. "You heard me."

They stood in the kitchen as Pen fixed dinner for the two of them. The film crew was leaving the next day for interior shooting in New York. Pen had a disconcerting and very painful sense of déjà vu about the conversation.

"Well, it's the stupidest thing you've ever done," Libby pronounced. "You broke up with him because you're afraid of getting hurt. Now you'll be miserable for the rest of your life, and he'll be miserable for the rest of his life. But that's better for both of you than trying to work out a life together? Grade A dumb!"

"You don't understand . . ." Pen began, shredding lettuce viciously.

"Hell, no, I don't." Libby snorted. "I thought I was the family's champ for avoiding commitment, but you make me look like a piker. You know what? I think for all your talk about being Richard's film fling, he was *your* summer fling."

Pen gasped in outrage. "That's a terrible thing to say!"

Libby shrugged. "Well, it looks that way to me."

"I think this conversation ought to end now," Pen suggested firmly.

"Quitting on this, too, eh? Well, that's not surprising. You quit on yourself and Richard. So hurry up with dinner. I don't have all night, you know."

Libby stomped out of the room. Pen cursed under her breath, picked up the rest of the head of lettuce she'd been shredding, and slammed the still-solid mass of it into the salad bowl.

"Dinner's served!"

"Are you going to let her get away with this?"

Richard glared at Libby. "What the hell do you mean?"

They were standing off to the side as the buses were being loaded with the luggage and equipment of those of the crew and cast still left in Blairstown. The academy's dormitory rose solid and stately behind them, sheltered by the canopy of trees in full leaf. Young women with pliant bodies, clear skin, and perfectly cut, shining hair gathered on the edges of the activity, watching and giggling. They only reminded Richard that a new school year was starting and he was leaving—without Pen.

"Aren't you going to fight for her?" Libby demanded. "Show her you love her?"

Richard set his jaw, knowing he'd already had this conversation once. With Pen. "I already did all that. It wasn't enough. She says her life is here, and a long-distance relationship wouldn't work."

"Ridiculous!"

"She says she can't live my fishbowl existence."

"Utter nonsense!"

"She says she can't stand even the idea of my doing love scenes."

"So tell her to go watch Robin Williams instead. Nobody's significant other watches the love scenes being filmed or shown in the theater."

"I told her that, dammit!" Richard exclaimed, pushing his fingers at his temples and pulling half his hair out of his ponytail in the process. "What it came down to was that I'm still the Cretin, Libby. She couldn't stand that."

His words brought silence. Finally Libby said in a very low, very shaken voice, "I can't believe Pen would ever even think such a thing, let alone say it."

"Of course she didn't *say* it!" Richard corrected. "She's too damn polite for that. But I know that's what it is. I thought I was past it, but I could tell—"

"Now, that is the biggest load of hogwash I have *ever* heard!" Libby glared at him. "In fact, it's plain old bull . . ." She finished the barnyard curse with relish. "The woman put you on a pedestal right from the beginning. She was gaga over you from the first. It was disgustingly mushy to see my cousin in such a state. She's crazy about you, but she's scared *she* won't measure up. So get your backside out there and show her how you feel about her. If you don't, you'll lose her forever."

"I told you—"

"Words, just words. It's action that counts. Figure out a way to *show* her it will work, and then do it!"

Libby stalked away. Richard stared after her. With a curse, he climbed onto the bus.

School had been in session almost two months when Pen came out to the parking lot to discover someone leaning against her car.

"Richard," she whispered, stopping dead. Teachers and late students flowed around her, staring curiously, but she didn't care.

All the agony of the past weeks without him were nothing compared to the pain coursing through her now. Her decision hadn't even begun to prepare her for the reality of not being with him. This was a mirage, she thought. Something her brain conjured up out of her unhappiness.

Slowly she moved, feeling like an old woman as she walked toward her car, positive the image would vanish the closer she got.

But it didn't. He wore sunglasses, plain black ones, and a baseball cap. The blue chambray shirt sat perfectly on his wide shoulders, sleeves rolled up to the elbows and revealing tanned forearms. His jeans were snug on his hips and legs, emphasizing that lean frame he had. The mocs were beat-up and, as always, he wore no socks.

But his hair was short.

Pen blinked. In her imagination he'd never once had short hair. She never would have even known how to envision him this way.

"You cut your hair," she said stupidly when she got close.

"It's all tucked up in the cap," he said. He straightened. "How are you?"

"Okay."

"How's Lolita?" He smiled slightly as he added, "I miss her."

He missed the cat. Not her. The cat. Pen forced herself not to show how much *that* hurt. "She's fine. How are you?"

"Fine."

He looked better than fine. He looked wonderful—too wonderful. Healthy and tanned, he clearly wasn't suffering over their breakup. She couldn't stand it, she thought, her body beginning to tremble. She couldn't walk away from him twice. She couldn't go through it again. She asked, "Why are you here?"

"There's something I want to show you," he answered. "Will you come with me?"

"Richard—"

"I just need an opinion on something, Pen. Please. It won't take long. I'll have you back here in an hour."

He was so calm, she thought dimly. And so distant. As if he didn't care about her any longer. Maybe he didn't.

That thought hurt worse than anything that had gone before.

He took her elbow. "My car's over here."

He led her like an automaton to a nondescript Buick.

"Where's the truck?" she asked as he opened the passenger door.

"Back at the dealership, I suppose." He tucked her into the seat. "It was a rental."

"Oh."

He slammed the door shut.

Pen closed her eyes, knowing she'd sounded incredibly dumb. In her worst moments, she had daydreamed about him coming back. None of them had her in a car, about to give him advice.

What if he wanted to ask her about another woman?

Get out of the car. Now! Pen put her hand on the door latch, but Richard was already climbing into the driver's seat. He started the car and pressed the automatic door locks. They snapped closed with a loud click.

"Where are we going?" Her voice was a hoarse croak, but she didn't bother to clear her throat or cover it up.

"Not far."

They drove in silence. She knew she was being incredibly foolish. But she couldn't help herself, either. She wanted to touch him, to fling herself into his arms, and she hated herself for the weakness.

"Here we are," he said after they had driven up Route 602 beyond Blairstown. He turned into a dirt track that wended its way back up the mountainside. He parked the car on the edge of a large glade, unlocked the car doors, and got out.

She followed silently.

"What do you think?" he asked.

"It's beautiful," she said. And it wasn't a lie. The trees allowed small shafts of light through, small beams of sun to dapple the mountain laurels, dogwoods and leafy underbrush. The foliage was already a burst of yellows and reds with the waxing of autumn. In a few weeks the ground would have a brown, rustling carpet of leaves, but for now the earth showed through, dark and rich, with the occasional fallen log as an inviting bench for the admirer.

In winter, Pen knew, the bare trees would permit a breathtaking view down the mountain. And then the snows would come, blanketing everything in a white fairyland. The pastels of flowering trees in the spring would be followed by the lush greens of summer. This place would show to perfection all its natural glories.

Richard walked over to her. He took off his sunglasses and looked at her somberly. His eyes were red, as if his nights were haunted. Like hers. "I'm building a house here."

She was astonished by the news. Her brain ran at lightning speed with a jumble of thoughts and images while her stomach clenched painfully, as if she'd been punched.

"I bought the property today," he continued. "I'm building my permanent home here."

How, she wondered desperately, was she to get over him, knowing he'd be living just up the road from her? It didn't matter that he'd be gone most of the time. Merely that he *owned* the place, that it would have his things inside, would be sheer torture.

"I wanted to know how you felt about it," he said. "Because you'll be living here too."

She blinked, then as the words penetrated, shook her head violently. "I can't live with you, Richard—"

"Well, I don't know of any other way married couples handle their lives."

She didn't hear him right, Pen thought dimly through the loud buzzing in her ears. Her vision went gray, and her brain seemed to disappear into a dark void.

"Married?" she croaked.

"Married. You getting a cold?"

"No. Richard, I can't marry you—"

"It's too late," he said. "I already booked a hall."

"You what?"

"I booked a hall. In Penns Grove, this morning, for next Saturday. And the invitations are going out . . ." He looked at his watch. "Probably they've gone out by now. You wouldn't believe how hard it is to get all that arranged, so I hope you don't mind that it's only immediate family and friends. About a hundred people. By the way, your parents said to say hello."

"My parents! You saw my parents?"

"Sure." He raised his eyebrows. "Pen, you can't exclude your parents from the wedding. What are you thinking of? By the way, my parents are looking forward to meeting you."

"Wait a minute!" she exclaimed, holding her head, half because of the confusion inside and half to keep the damn thing on her shoulders. "Just wait a minute! You arranged a wedding—"

"I may be a man, but I'm not incapable of it," he interrupted.

"*Our* wedding?"

"It wasn't Harry and Sally's. If I waited for you to do it, hell would freeze over first. We're going to have to get our blood tests done and get the certificate right away, otherwise we'll have to do it again in a civil service." He slashed the air with his hand. "Dammit, Pen! I can't stand this! You're going to have to be miserable and unhappy with me, because I can't live without you. I don't know how else to show you where I want to be . . . I need to be . . . except to do it. And if you won't marry me, I'll haunt you. I'll be in your face every chance I get. I'll be right here for the rest of my life, because this is where *I* want to live. You won't ever get away from me again, so surrender now and put yourself out of your misery. I'm not the Cretin anymore, Pen. This time I'm the bully. For both our sakes."

"Richard . . ." She started to cry.

He muttered a curse, then pulled her into his arms against the solid wall of his chest. She buried her face in the cotton material and wept.

"Please, Pen," he said in a low voice, a voice that was breaking with his own emotions. "I can't stand us not even trying. We have to try. I don't want the Hollywood fishbowl existence, either. This is where I want to have my family. This is where my values are. I need this to renew myself and my craft. I'll travel some, but I'd do that anyway because most films are shot on location now. Maybe sometimes you can come with me, sometimes not. We'll work through those times. Together. I talked to Cindy Costner about love scenes. She's like you, Pen, not another actor. She says she'll be happy to talk with you about how to handle them. I know it won't be easy, but that's what makes you all the more important to me. I love you. I *have* to marry you. I want vows to me you can't ever break, and I want vows to you I can't ever break. It'll kill me if I don't."

"I think I'm dreaming again," she finally murmured, lifting her head.

He kissed her, an earth-shattering kiss of longings and yearnings and promises. When he let her mouth go, he grinned. "No dream. Solid reality, babe."

"Oh, Lord, you have been in Hollywood." She sobered. "I love you, Richard. I'm scared, but I can't be without you anymore. It's a shadow life, worthless."

"Do you really like this place?" he asked. "If you don't, we can buy another piece of land—"

"No." She snuggled closer, content. "Did you really see my parents and arrange our wedding?"

"A week from Saturday." He chuckled.

"I'm going to have to speak to you about this chauvinistic streak of yours. Eventually."

"Eventually." His fingers started unbuttoning her shirt.

"I thought we had a license to get," she reminded him a little breathlessly as his warm knuckles slid along her bared skin.

"Tomorrow's good enough. Besides, we have to have our priorities straight. I haven't seen the whole view yet."

"Did you really talk to *the* Cindy Costner?" she asked, wanting only to get rid of the last plaguing questions before getting down to important matters.

"One and the same." He pulled the shirt from her shoulders. As he hooked his thumbs under her bra straps and simply pulled them down over her arms, dispensing with the undergarment, he added, "Nice lady. She reminded me of you."

Pen reached up and flipped his cap off. The familiar ponytail tumbled out. She wrapped her fingers in the heavy strands and brought his mouth down to hers for a devastating kiss. Feminine power and emotional security were flowing through her in great cresting waves. At last she broke the kiss and asked, "Now, who were you talking about?"

"I have no idea," he admitted.

"Your heart is mine, your mouth is mine, your soul is mine, your body is mine, and what's under your loincloth is *definitely* mine. And don't you for-get it."

"I love you too," he said, and pulled her down under the trees of their future home.

EPILOGUE

The Academy Awards were always a glittering affair.

Richard grimaced as he walked the gauntlet of reporters, blaring lights, and the all-seeing eyes of the television cameras. Fans screamed from the grandstand, trying to get his attention. He waved cheerfully to them, grateful that they had kept *American Saga* number one at the box office for three months, earning it over $100 million, earning it nine Oscar nominations.

"You're remarkably relaxed for a nominee," Pen muttered, her fingers digging into the crook of his arm. "I'm a nervous wreck for you."

He chuckled and adjusted his glasses. He remembered when she had rescued his glasses so long ago. Who would have guessed then that they would be together, let alone where they were now? His nomination should have made him feel vindicated for all those school tormentors, but, in truth, it didn't even matter anymore and hadn't for a long time. He renewed himself in his mountaintop home, knowing himself for a person of true worth. He had a rich life, which he felt he deserved because he worked at it. Everything else was gravy, and an Oscar nomination was fantastic gravy.

"Hell, honey, I'm just honored to have been nominated. Nicholson surpassed Spencer Tracy and Bette Davis for the most nominations ever. They didn't give it to him for *Hoffa* or *A Few Good Men*, so he'll get it this time. And he deserves it. It was a brilliant performance." He squeezed her hand. "Now you know how I felt when you got the New Jersey Teacher of the Year award."

She laughed. "For my classes on filming *your* movie."

"You look beautiful." And she did. Her strapless gown of dark blue chiffon had been lent by Chanel. Little stars streamed across the material, as if flung by an unseen hand in a lovely arc of shimmering silver. Her hair was pulled back in a heavy chignon at her nape. She would have held her own with the glamorous stars of Hollywood's early years. But the real beauty was inside her, their baby still small and secret. Pregnancy made her stunning.

She grinned at him. "So do you. But I still miss the hair."

He chuckled. "I'll have to let it grow again. After this part."

He was testing his acting in an entirely different direction with a screwball comedy. Despite the truth of Burke's deathbed words that acting was easy and comedy hard, he was having fun too. All because of Pen. Because of the emotional foundation she provided with her love.

It wasn't easy for them. She traveled with him when school was out, and he used the red-eye to get home as many weekends as he could while school was in.

The "Entertainment Tonight" staging-area people waved him over for an interview. They were joined by Libby, who was ebullient. She had a right to be, with a director's nomination under her belt. She'd already won the Golden Globe.

She hugged Pen, then him. "You look happy, and you can thank me for it."

"What is she talking about?" Pen asked.

Richard shrugged. "She's your cousin."

"Direction, kiddies. Subtle direction to get you two back together. You're up, Richard."

That was last night, he thought with a private grin to his wife, but went for his interview like a dutiful son.

After that they were whisked inside to their seats in the pavilion. The show was its usual combination of overdone glitz, boorish political statements, tedious scripting, and expected winners. Libby was sitting next to them, muttering about the Academy being better off getting Attila the Hun to direct.

"I'll volunteer you for next year," Pen muttered, effectively shutting her cousin up. Richard raised her hand and kissed it. She was doing well for the fishbowl.

Even as the announcements got closer to the final four, *Saga* hadn't pulled anything yet. Pen cursed at each pass-over for the movie. Libby was practically incoherent. Richard checked his nerves and found them completely calm. It was nice to know he hadn't a chance.

Mary Jane got the award for Best Actress.

He was on his feet, clapping furiously for his costar, as were Pen and Libby, who was also whistling between her fingers. To his surprise, when Mary Jane gave her acceptance speech, one of the people she thanked was Pen.

"What *did* you say to Mary Jane?" he asked.

"I told you: that she was a great actress." Pen grinned.

Everyone settled again, enduring yet another film clip on the show's theme. But anticipation was mounting for the next award.

"Please, please, please, please," Pen chanted like a mantra.

"Relax, love," Richard told her, amused and grateful. "It's a wonderful thought, but I don't have a snowball's chance in hell. Besides, I have you. And the baby."

Pen smiled at him, the love shining out of her eyes. "You have more than a snowball's chance in hell. You were brilliant."

"Better than Nicholson," Libby murmured to him across Pen. "You had better direction."

Pen looked heavenward for help. "She's insufferable."

Finally they got to the Best Actor. Al Pacino and Emma Thompson strode onstage to present the award. As the nominees were read and a clip of their individual performances shown, Richard felt a twinge of hope, followed immediately by the knowledge of loss. It was his first nomination. There would be more. He hoped. But it was nice to have the pressure off.

He felt the lights focus on him as his name was announced as a nominee. He smiled and tried not to think of a billion people watching. Pen's fingers entwined with his and squeezed in reassurance.

His heart sank as they showed a clip of the big love scene with Mary Jane. To his relief, Pen sighed when it was over and said, "That was the greatest acting I ever saw. It still is."

Richard leaned over and kissed her. "I love you."

"And the winner is . . ."

The envelope rattled as it was torn open. Richard relaxed back in his chair, content with his life. Nothing could top it.

"Richard Creighton. *American Saga*."

Pen flung herself at him, her arms literally cutting off his air as she spread kisses all over his cheek and ear. She was screaming his name at the same time. Libby's voice was whooping in the distance. It occurred to him that he actually had won as a ripple of amusement went through the audience at his wife's antics. He had won!

"Get up! Get up!" Pen suddenly shouted, urging him out of his seat and down the aisle to the stage.

They put the statue in his hands, and he stared at it for a long moment, positive it had been a big mistake. Then he turned to the microphone, knowing he had a lot of people to thank and only a few seconds in which to do it. He saved the best for last.

" . . . I can never thank the most important person in my life enough. My wife, Pen Marsh-Creighton. Even though she just tried to kiss me to death . . ." People chuckled. Richard grinned at he stared up through the sea of faces to unerringly find his wife's. " . . . No one could ever receive the kind of wonderful support, encouragement and love she's given to me. I share this with her. Thank you." As the director sliced his finger across his throat, signaling his time was up, Richard added, "Okay, Libby, let's hope this is a real family night!"

As Libby and *American Saga* made the Oscar sweep,

Richard admitted he had shown a billion people what a totally and disgustingly and happily married man he was.

But Pen already knew that.

THE EDITOR'S CORNER

Celebrate the most romantic month of the year with LOVESWEPT! In the six fabulous novels coming your way, you'll thrill to the sexiest heroes and cheer for the most spirited heroines as they discover the power of passion. It's all guaranteed to get you in the mood for love.

Starting the lineup is the ever-popular Fayrene Preston with **STORM SONG**, LOVESWEPT #666—and Noah McKane certainly comes across like a force of nature. He's the hottest act in town, but he never gives interviews, never lets anyone get close to him—until Cate Gallin persuades the powerfully sensual singer to let her capture him on film. Nobody knows the secret they share, the bonds of pain and emotion that go soul-deep . . . or the risks they're taking when Cate accepts the challenge to reveal his stunning talent—without hurting the only man she's ever loved. This compelling novel is proof positive of why Fayrene is one of the best-loved authors of the genre.

SLIGHTLY SHADY by Jan Hudson, LOVE-SWEPT #667, is Maggie Marino's first impression of the brooding desperado she sees in the run-down bar. On the run from powerful forces, she's gotten stranded deep in the heart of Texas, and the last thing she wants is to tangle with a mesmerizing outlaw who calls himself Shade. But Shade knows just how to comfort a woman, and Maggie soon finds herself surrendering to his sizzling looks—even as she wonders what secret he's hiding. To tantalize you even further, we'll tell you that Shade is truly Paul Berringer, a tiger of the business world and brother of the Berringer twins who captivated you in **BIG AND BRIGHT** and **CALL ME SIN**. So don't miss out on Paul's own story. Bad boys don't come any better, and as usual Jan Hudson's writing shines with humor and sizzles with sensuality.

Please give a warm welcome to Gayle Kasper and her very first LOVESWEPT, **TENDER, LOVING CURE**, #668. As you may have guessed, this utterly delightful romance features a doctor, and there isn't a finer one than Joel Benedict. He'd do anything to become even better—except attend a sex talk seminar. He changes his mind, though, when he catches a glimpse of the teacher. Maggie Springer is a temptress who makes Joel think of private lessons, and when a taste of her kissable lips sparks the fire beneath his cool facade, he starts to believe that it's possible for him to love once more. We're happy to be Gayle's publisher, and this terrific novel will show you why.

Sally Goldenbaum returns to LOVESWEPT with **MOONLIGHT ON MONTEREY BAY**, #669. The beach in that part of California has always been special to Sam Eastland, and when he goes to his empty house there, he doesn't expect to discover a beautiful nymph. Interior decorator Maddie Ames fights to convince him that only she can create a sanctuary to soothe his troubled spirit . . . and he's too spellbound to refuse. But when their attraction flares into burning passion and Sam fears he can't give Maddie the joy she deserves, she must persuade him not to underestimate the power of love. Vibrant with heartfelt emotion, this romance showcases Sally's evocative writing. Welcome back, Sally!

A spooky manor house, things that go bump in the night—all this and more await you in **MIDNIGHT LADY**, LOVESWEPT #670, by Linda Wisdom. The granddaughter of the king of horror movies, Samantha Lyons knows all about scare tactics, and she uses them to try to keep Kyle Fletcher from getting the inside scoop about her family's film studio. But the devastatingly handsome reporter isn't about to abandon the story—or break the sensual magic that has woven itself around him and beautiful Sam . . . even if wooing her means facing down ghosts! Hold on to your seats because Linda is about to take you on a roller-coaster ride of dangerous desires and exquisite sensations.

It **LOOKS LIKE LOVE** when Drew Webster first sees Jill Stuart in Susan Connell's new LOVESWEPT, #671. Jill is a delicious early-morning surprise, clad in silky lingerie, kneeling in Drew's uncle's yard, and coaxing a puppy into her arms. Drew knows instantly that she wouldn't have to beg him to come running, and he sets off on a passionate courtship. To Jill, temptation has never looked or felt so good, but when Drew insists that there's a thief in the retirement community she manages, she tells him it can't be true, that she has everything under control. Drew wants to trust her, but can he believe the angel who's stolen his heart?

Susan delivers a wonderful love story that will warm your heart.

Happy reading!

With warmest wishes,

Nita Taublib

Nita Taublib

Associate Publisher

P.S. Don't miss the exciting women's novels from Bantam that are coming your way in February—**THE BELOVED SCOUNDREL** by nationally bestselling author Iris Johansen, a tempestuous tale of abduction, seduction, and surrender that sweeps from the shimmering halls of Regency England to the decadent haunts of a notorious rogue; **VIXEN** by award-winning author Jane Feather, a spectacular historical romance in which an iron-willed nobleman suddenly becomes the guardian of a mischievous, orphaned beauty; and **ONE FINE DAY** by supertalented Theresa Weir, which tells the searing story of a second chance for happiness for Molly and Austin Bennet, two memorable characters from Theresa's previous novel **FOREVER**. We'll be giving you a sneak peek at these terrific books in next month's LOVESWEPTs. And immediately following this page look for a preview of the exciting romances from Bantam that are *available now!*

Don't miss these exciting books by your
favorite Bantam authors

On sale in December:

DESIRE
by Amanda Quick

LONG TIME COMING
by Sandra Brown

STRANGER IN MY ARMS
by R.J. Kaiser

WHERE DOLPHINS GO
by Peggy Webb

And in hardcover from Doubleday
AMAZON LILY
by Theresa Weir

"One of the hottest and most prolific writers in romance today . . . Her heroines are always spunky women you'd love to know, and her heroes are dashing guys you'd love to love."
—*USA Today*

Amanda Quick

New York Times bestselling author of **DANGEROUS** and **DECEPTION**

DESIRE

This spectacular novel is Amanda Quick's first medieval romance!

From the windswept, craggy coast of a remote British isle comes the thrilling tale of a daring lady and a dangerous knight who are bound by the tempests of fate and by the dawning of desire . . .

"There was something you wished to discuss with me, sir?"

"Aye. Our marriage."

Clare flinched, but she did not fall off the bench. Under the circumstances, she considered that a great accomplishment. "You are very direct about matters, sir."

He looked mildly surprised. "I see no point in being otherwise."

"Nor do I. Very well, sir, let me be blunt. In spite of your efforts to establish yourself in everyone's eyes as the sole suitor for my hand, I must tell you again that your expectations are unrealistic."

"Nay, madam," Gareth said very quietly. "'Tis your expectations that are unrealistic. I read the letter you sent to Lord Thurston. It is obvious you hope to marry a phantom, a man who does not exist. I fear you must settle for something less than perfection."

She lifted her chin. "You think that no man can be found who suits my requirements?"

"I believe that we are both old enough and wise enough to know that marriage is a practical matter. It has nothing to do with the passions that the troubadours make so much of in their foolish ballads."

Clare clasped her hands together very tightly. "Kindly do not condescend to lecture me on the subject of marriage, sir. I am only too well aware that in my case it is a matter of duty, not desire. But in truth, when I composed my recipe for a husband, I did not believe that I was asking for so very much."

"Mayhap you will discover enough good points in me to satisfy you, madam."

Clare blinked. "Do you actually believe that?"

"I would ask you to examine closely what I have to offer. I think that I can meet a goodly portion of your requirements."

She surveyed him from head to toe. "You most definitely do not meet my requirements in the matter of size."

"Concerning my size, as I said earlier, there is little I can do about it, but I assure you I do not generally rely upon it to obtain my ends."

Clare gave a ladylike snort of disbelief.

"'Tis true. I prefer to use my wits rather than muscle whenever possible."

"Sir, I shall be frank. I want a man of peace for this isle. Desire has never known violence. I intend to keep things that way. I do not want a husband who thrives on the sport of war."

He looked down at her with an expression of surprise. "I have no love of violence or war."

Clare raised her brows. "Are you going to tell me that you have no interest in either? You, who carry a sword with a terrible name? You, who wear a reputation as a destroyer of murderers and thieves?"

"I did not say I had no interest in such matters. I have, after all, used a warrior's skills to make my way in the world. They are the tools of my trade, that's all."

"A fine point, sir."

"But a valid one. I have grown weary of violence, madam. I seek a quiet, peaceful life."

Clare did not bother to hide her skepticism. "An interesting statement, given your choice of career."

"I did not have much choice in the matter of my career," Gareth said. "Did you?"

"Nay, but that is—"

"Let us go on to your second requirement. You wrote that you desire a man of cheerful countenance and even temperament."

She stared at him, astonished. "You consider yourself a man of cheerful countenance?"

"Nay, I admit that I have been told my countenance is somewhat less than cheerful. But I am most definitely a man of even temperament."

"I do not believe that for a moment, sir."

"I promise you, it is the truth. You may inquire of anyone who knows me. Ask Sir Ulrich. He has been my companion for years. He will tell you that I am the most even-tempered of men. I am not given to fits of rage or foul temper."

Or to mirth and laughter, either, Clare thought as she met his smoky crystal eyes. "Very well, I shall grant that you may be even-tempered in a certain sense, although that was not quite what I had in mind."

"You see? We are making progress here." Gareth reached up to grasp a limb of the apple tree. "Now, then, to continue. Regarding your last requirement, I remind you yet again that I can read."

Clare cast about frantically for a fresh tactic. "Enough, sir. I grant that you meet a small number of my requirements if one interprets them very broadly. But what about our own? Surely there are some specific things you seek in a wife."

"My requirements?" Gareth looked taken back by the question. "My requirements in a wife are simple, madam. I believe that you will satisfy them."

"Because I hold lands and the recipes of a plump perfume business? Think twice before you decide that is sufficient to satisfy you sir. We live a simple life here on Desire. Quite boring in most respects. You are a man who is no doubt accustomed to the grand entertainments provided in the households of great lords."

"I can do without such entertainments, my lady. They hold no appeal for me."

"You have obviously lived an adventurous, exciting life," Clare persisted. "Will you find contentment in the business of growing flowers and making perfumes?"

"Aye, madam, I will," Gareth said with soft satisfaction.

"'Tis hardly a career suited to a knight of your reputation, sir."

"Rest assured that here on Desire I expect to find the things that are most important to me."

Clare lost patience with his reasonableness. "And just what are those things, sir?"

"Lands, a hall of my own, and a woman who can give me a family." Gareth reached down and pulled her to her feet as effortlessly as though she were fashioned of thistledown. "You can provide me with all of those things, lady. That makes you very valuable to me. Do not imagine that I will not protect you well. And do not think that I will let you slip out of my grasp."

"But—"

Gareth brought his mouth down on hers, silencing her protest.

LONG TIME COMING
by

SANDRA BROWN

Blockbuster author Sandra Brown—whose name is almost synonymous with the *New York Times* bestseller list—offers up a classic romantic novel that aches with emotion and sizzles with passion . . .

For sixteen years Marnie Hibbs had raised her sister's son as her own, hoping that her love would make up for the father David would never know . . . dreaming that someday David's father would find his way back into her life. And then one afternoon Marnie looked up and Law Kincaid was there, as strong and heartbreakingly handsome as ever. Flooded with bittersweet memories, Marnie yearned to lose herself in his arms, yet a desperate fear held her back, for this glorious man who had given her David now had the power to take him away. . . .

The Porsche crept along the street like a sleek black panther. Hugging the curb, its engine purred so deep and low it sounded like a predator's growl.

Marnie Hibbs was kneeling in the fertile soil of her flower bed, digging among the impatiens under the ligustrum bushes and cursing the little bugs that made three meals a day of them, when the sound of the car's motor attracted her attention. She glanced at it over her shoulder, then panicked as it came to a stop in front of her house.

"Lord, is it that late?" she muttered. Dropping her trowel, she stood up and brushed the clinging damp earth off her bare knees.

She reached up to push her dark bangs off her forehead before she realized that she still had on her heavy gardening gloves. Quickly she peeled them off and dropped them beside the trowel, all the while watching the driver get out of the sports car and start up her front walk.

Glancing at her wristwatch, she saw that she hadn't lost track of time. He was just very early for their appointment, and as a result, she wasn't going to make a very good first impression. Being hot, sweaty, and dirty was no way to meet a client. And she needed this commission badly.

Forcing a smile, she moved down the sidewalk to greet him, nervously trying to remember if she had left the house and studio reasonably neat when she decided to do an hour's worth of yard work. She had planned to tidy up before he arrived.

She might look like the devil, but she didn't want to appear intimidated. Self-confident friendliness was the only way to combat the disadvantage of having been caught looking her worst.

He was still several yards away from her when she greeted him. "Hello," she said with a bright smile. "Obviously we got our signals switched. I thought you weren't coming until later."

"I decided this diabolical game of yours had gone on long enough."

Marnie's sneakers skidded on the old concrete walk as she came to an abrupt halt. She tilted her head in stunned surprise. "I'm sorry, I—"

"Who the hell are you, lady?"

"Miss Hibbs. Who do you think?"

"Never heard of you. Just what the devil are you up to?"

"Up to?" She glanced around helplessly, as though the giant sycamores in her front yard might provide an answer to this bizarre interrogation.

"Why've you been sending me those letters?"

"Letters?"

He was clearly furious, and her lack of comprehension only seemed to make him angrier. He bore down on her like a hawk on a field mouse, until she had to bow her back to look up at him. The summer sun was behind him, casting him in silhouette.

He was blond, tall, trim, and dressed in casual slacks and a sport shirt—all stylish, impeccably so. He was wearing opaque aviator glasses, so she couldn't see his eyes, but if they were as belligerent as his expression and stance, she was better off not seeing them.

"I don't know what you're talking about."

"The letters, lady, the letters." He strained the words through a set of strong white teeth.

"*What* letters?"

"Don't play dumb."

"Are you sure you've got the right house?"

He took another step forward. "I've got the right house," he said in a voice that was little more than a snarl.

"Obviously you don't." She didn't like being put on the defensive, especially by someone she'd never met over something of which she was totally ignorant. "You're either crazy or drunk, but in any case, you're *wrong*. I'm not the person you're looking for and I demand that you leave my property. Now."

"You were expecting me. I could tell by the way you spoke to me."

"I thought you were the man from the advertising agency."

"Well, I'm not."

"Thank God." She would hate having to do business with someone this irrational and ill-tempered.

"You know damn well who I am," he said, peeling off the sunglasses.

Marnie sucked in a quick, sharp breath and fell back a step because she did indeed know who he was. She raised a hand to her chest in an attempt at keeping her jumping heart in place. "Law," she gasped.

"That's right. Law Kincaid. Just like you wrote it on the envelopes."

She was shocked to see him after all these years, standing only inches in front of her. This time he wasn't merely a familiar image in the newspaper or on her television screen. He was flesh and blood. The years had been kind to that flesh, improving his looks, not eroding them.

She wanted to stand and stare, but he was staring at her with unmitigated contempt and no recognition at all. "Let's go inside, Mr. Kincaid," she suggested softly.

STRANGER IN MY ARMS
by
R.J. KAISER

With the chilling tension of Hitchcock and the passionate heat of Sandra Brown, STRANGER IN MY ARMS is a riveting novel of romantic suspense in which a woman with amnesia suspects she is a target for murder.

Here is a look at this powerful novel . . .

"Tell me who you are, Carter, where you came from, about your past—everything."

He complied, giving me a modest summary of his life. He'd started his career in New York and formed a partnership with a British firm in London. When his partners suffered financial difficulties, he convinced my father to buy them out. Altogether he'd been in Europe for twelve years.

Carter was forty, ten years older than I. He'd been born and raised in Virginia, where his parents still resided. He'd attended Dartmouth and the Harvard Business School. In addition to the villa he had a house in Kensington, a flat off the avenue Bosquet in Paris, and a small farm outside Charlottesville, Virginia.

After completing his discourse, he leaned back and sipped his coffee. I watched him while Yvonne cleared the table.

Carter Bass was an attractive man with sophistication and class. He was well-spoken, educated. But mainly he appealed to me because I felt a connection with him, tortured though it was. We'd been dancing around each other since he'd appeared on the scene, our history at war with our more immediate and intangible feelings toward each other.

I could only assume that the allure he held for me had to do with the fact that he was both a stranger and my husband. My body, in effect, remembered Carter as my mind could not.

I picked up my coffee cup, but paused with it at my lips. Something had been troubling me for some time and I decided to blurt it out. "Do you have a mistress, Carter?"

He blinked. "What kind of a question is that?"

"A serious one. You know all about me, it's only fair I know about you."

"I don't have a mistress."

"Are you lonely?"

He smiled indulgently. "Hillary, we have an unspoken agreement. You don't ask and neither do I."

"Then you don't want to talk about it? I should mind my own business, is that what you mean?"

He contemplated me. "Maybe we should step out onto the terrace for some air—sort of clear our mental palate."

"If you like."

Carter came round and helped me up. "Could I interest you in a brandy?"

"I don't think so. I enjoyed the wine. That's really all I'd like."

He took my arm and we went through the salon and onto the terrace. He kept his hand on my elbow, though I was no longer shaky. His attention was flattering, and I decided I liked the changing chemistry between us, even though I had so many doubts.

It was a clear night and there were countless stars. I inhaled the pleasantly cool air and looked at my husband. Carter let his hand drop away.

"I miss this place," he said.

"Did I drive you away?"

"No, I've stayed away by choice."

"It's all so sad," I said, staring off down the dark valley. "I think we're a tragic pair. People shouldn't be as unhappy as we seem to be."

"You're talking about the past. Amnesiacs aren't supposed to do that, my dear."

I smiled at his teasing.

"I'm learning all about myself, about us, very quickly."

"I wonder if you're better off not knowing," he said, a trace of sadness in his voice.

"I can't run away from who I am," I replied.

"No, I suppose you can't."

"You'd like for me to change, though, wouldn't you?"

"What difference does it make? Your condition is temporary. It's probably better in the long run to treat you as the person I know you to be."

His words seemed cruel—or at least unkind—though what he was saying was not only obvious, it was also reasonable. Why should he assume the burden of my sins? I sighed and looked away.

"I'd like to believe in you, Hillary," he said. "But it isn't as simple as just giving you the benefit of the doubt."

"If I could erase the past, I would." My eyes shimmered. "But even if you were willing, *they* wouldn't let me."

Carter knew whom I was referring to. "They" were the police, and "they" were coming for me in the morning, though their purpose was still somewhat vague. "They" were the whole issue, it seemed to me—maybe the final arbiter of who I really was. My past not only defined me, it was my destiny.

"I don't think you should jump to any conclusions," he said. "Let's wait and see what they have to say."

He reached out and took my bare arms, seemingly to savor the feel of my skin. His hands were quite warm, and he gripped me firmly as he searched my eyes. I was sure then that he had brought me to the terrace to touch me, to connect with me physically. He had wanted to be close to me. And maybe I'd come along because I wanted to be close to him.

There were signs of desire in Carter's eyes. Heat. My heart picked up its beat when he lowered his mouth toward mine. His kiss was tender and it aroused me. I'd hungered for this—for the affirmation, for the affection—more than I knew. But still I wasn't prepared for it. I didn't expect to want him as much as I did.

I kissed Carter every bit as deeply as he kissed me. Then, at exactly the same moment, we pulled apart, retreating as swiftly as we'd come together. When I looked into his eyes I saw the reflection of my own feelings—the same doubt, distrust, and fear that I myself felt.

And when he released me, I realized that the issues separating us remained unresolved. The past, like the future, was undeniable. The morning would come. It would come much too soon.

WHERE DOLPHINS GO
by
PEGGY WEBB

"Ms. Webb has an inventive mind brimming
with originality that makes all of her books
special reading."
—*Romantic Times*

*To Susan Riley, the dolphins at the Oceanfront Research Center
were her last chance to reach her frail, broken child. Yet when she
brought Jeffy to the Center, she never expected to have to contend
with a prickly doctor who made it clear that he didn't intend to
get involved. Quiet, handsome, and hostile, Paul Taylor was a
wounded man, and when Susan learned of the tragedy behind his
anguish, she knew she had to help. But what began as compassion
soon turned to desire, and now Susan was falling for a man who
belonged to someone else. . . .*

"A woman came to see me today," Bill said. "A woman and
a little boy."

Paul went very still.

"Her name is Susan . . . Susan Riley. She knew about the
center from that article in the newspaper last week."

There had been many articles written about Dr. Bill
McKenzie and the research he did with dolphins. The most
recent one, though, had delved into the personality of the
dolphins themselves. An enterprising reporter had done his
homework. "Dolphins," he had written, "relate well to people. Some even seem to have extrasensory perception. They
seem to sense when a person is sick or hurt or depressed."

"Her little boy has a condition called truncus arteriosus . . ." Bill squinted in the way he always did when he
was judging a person's reaction.

Paul was careful not to show one. *Truncus arteriosus. A condition of the heart. Malfunctioning arteries. Surgery required.*

"Bill, I don't practice medicine anymore."

"I'm not asking you to practice medicine. I'm asking you to listen."

"I'm listening."

"The boy was scheduled for surgery, but he had a stroke before it could be performed."

For God's sake, Paul. Do something. DO SOMETHING!

"Bill . . ."

"The child is depressed, doesn't respond to anything, anybody. She thought the dolphins might be the answer. She wanted to bring him here on a regular basis."

"You told her no, of course."

"I'm a marine biologist, not a psychologist." Bill slumped in his chair. "I told her no."

"The child needs therapy, not dolphins."

"That's what I thought, but now . . ." Bill gave Paul that squinty-eyed look. "You're a doctor, Paul. Maybe if I let her bring the boy here during feeding times—"

"No. Dammit, Bill. Look at me. I can't even help myself, let alone a dying child and a desperate mother."

Bill looked down at his shoes and counted to ten under his breath. When he looked up Paul could see the pity in his eyes.

He hated that most of all. . . .

Susan hadn't meant to cry.

She knew before she came to the Oceanfront Research Center that her chances of success were slim. And yet she had to try. She couldn't live with herself if she didn't do everything in her power to help Jeffy.

Her face was already wet with tears as she lifted her child from his stroller and placed him in the car. He was so lifeless, almost as if he had already died and had forgotten to take his body with him. When she bent over him to fasten the seat belt, her tears dripped onto his still face.

He didn't even notice.

She swiped at her tears, mad at herself. Crying wasn't going to help Jeffy. Crying wasn't going to help either of them.

Resolutely she folded the stroller and put it in the backseat. Then she blew her nose and climbed into the driver's seat. Couldn't let Jeffy know she was sad. Did he see? Did he know?

The doctors had assured her that he did. That the stroke damage had been confined to areas of the brain that affected his motor control. That his bright little mind and his personality were untouched. And yet, he sat beside her like some discarded rag doll, staring at nothing.

Fighting hard against the helpless feeling she sometimes got when she looked at Jeffy, she turned the key in the ignition and waited for the old engine to warm up. She was not helpless. And she refused to let herself become that way.

"Remember that little song you love so much, Jeffy? The one Mommy wrote?" Jeffy stared at his small sneakers.

Sweat plastered Susan's hair to the sides of her face and made the back of her sundress stick to the seat.

"Mommy's going to sing it to you, darling, while we drive." She put the car into gear and backed out of the parking space, giving herself time to get the quiver out of her voice. She was *not* going to cry again. "You remember the words, don't you, sweetheart? Help Mommy sing, Jeffy."

" 'Sing with a voice of gladness; sing with a voice of joy.' " Susan's voice was neither glad nor joyful, but at least it no longer quivered. Control was easier in the daytime. It was at night, lying in the dark all by herself, when she lost it. She had cried herself to sleep many nights, muffling the sounds in the pillow in case Jeffy, sleeping in the next room, could hear.

" 'Shout for the times of goodness.' " How many good times could Jeffy remember? " 'Shout for the time of cheer.' " How many happy times had he had? Born with a heart condition, he had missed the ordinary joys other children took for granted—chasing a dog, kicking a ball, tumbling in the leaves, outrunning the wind.

" 'Sing with a voice that's hopeful . . . ' " Susan sang on, determined to be brave, determined to bring her child back from that dark, silent world he had entered.

As the car took a curve, Jeffy's head lolled to the side so he was staring straight at her. All the brightness of childhood that should be in his eyes was dulled over by four years of pain and defeat.

Why do you let me hurt?

The message in those eyes made her heart break.

The song died on her lips, the last clear notes lingering in the car like a party guest who didn't know it was time to go home. Susan turned her head to look out the window.

Biloxi was parching under the late afternoon sun. Dust devils shimmered in the streets. Palm trees, sagging and dusty, looked as tired as she felt. It seemed years since she had had a peaceful night's sleep. An eternity since she had had a day of fun and relaxation.

She was selfish to the core. Thinking about her own needs, her own desires. She had to think about Jeffy. There must be something that would spark his interest besides the dolphins.

And don't miss these heart-stopping
romances from Bantam Books,
on sale in January

THE BELOVED SCOUNDREL
by the nationally bestselling author
Iris Johansen
"You'll be riveted from beginning to end
as [Iris Johansen] holds you captive to a
love story of grand proportions."
—*Romantic Times* on
The Magnificent Rogue

VIXEN
by **Jane Feather**
A passionate tale of an iron-willed
nobleman who suddenly becomes the
guardian of a mischievous, orphaned
beauty.

ONE FINE DAY
by **Theresa Weir**
"Theresa Weir's writing is poignant,
passionate and powerful. *One Fine Day*
delivers intense emotion and compelling
characters that will capture the
hearts of readers."
—*New York Times* bestselling
author Jayne Ann Krentz

OFFICIAL RULES

To enter the sweepstakes below carefully follow all instructions found elsewhere in this offer.

The **Winners Classic** will award prizes with the following approximate maximum values: 1 Grand Prize: $26,500 (or $25,000 cash alternate); 1 First Prize: $3,000; 5 Second Prizes: $400 each; 35 Third Prizes: $100 each; 1,000 Fourth Prizes: $7.50 each. Total maximum retail value of Winners Classic Sweepstakes is $42,500. Some presentations of this sweepstakes may contain individual entry numbers corresponding to one or more of the aforementioned prize levels. To determine the Winners, individual entry numbers will first be compared with the winning numbers preselected by computer. For winning numbers not returned, prizes will be awarded in random drawings from among all eligible entries received. Prize choices may be offered at various levels. If a winner chooses an automobile prize, all license and registration fees, taxes, destination charges and, other expenses not offered herein are the responsibility of the winner. If a winner chooses a trip, travel must be complete within one year from the time the prize is awarded. Minors must be accompanied by an adult. Travel companion(s) must also sign release of liability. Trips are subject to space and departure availability. Certain black-out dates may apply.

The following applies to the sweepstakes named above:

No purchase necessary. You can also enter the sweepstakes by sending your name and address to: P.O. Box 508, Gibbstown, N.J. 08027. Mail each entry separately. Sweepstakes begins 6/1/93. Entries must be received by 12/30/94. Not responsible for lost, late, damaged, misdirected, illegible or postage due mail. Mechanically reproduced entries are not eligible. All entries become property of the sponsor and will not be returned.

Prize Selection/Validations: Selection of winners will be conducted no later than 5:00 PM on January 28, 1995, by an independent judging organization whose decisions are final. Random drawings will be held at 1211 Avenue of the Americas, New York, N.Y. 10036. Entrants need not be present to win. Odds of winning are determined by total number of entries received. Circulation of this sweepstakes is estimated not to exceed 200 million. All prizes are guaranteed to be awarded and delivered to winners. Winners will be notified by mail and may be required to complete an affidavit of eligibility and release of liability which must be returned within 14 days of date on notification or alternate winners will be selected in a random drawing. Any prize notification letter or any prize returned to a participating sponsor, Bantam Doubleday Dell Publishing Group, Inc., its participating divisions or subsidiaries, or the independent judging organization as undeliverable will be awarded to an alternate winner. Prizes are not transferable. No substitution for prizes except as offered or as may be necessary due to unavailability, in which case a prize of equal or greater value will be awarded. Prizes will be awarded approximately 90 days after the drawing. All taxes are the sole responsibility of the winners. Entry constitutes permission (except where prohibited by law) to use winners' names, hometowns, and likenesses for publicity purposes without further or other compensation. Prizes won by minors will be awarded in the name of parent or legal guardian.

Participation: Sweepstakes open to residents of the United States and Canada, except for the province of Quebec. Sweepstakes sponsored by Bantam Doubleday Dell Publishing Group, Inc., (BDD), 1540 Broadway, New York, NY 10036. Versions of this sweepstakes with different graphics and prize choices will be offered in conjunction with various solicitations or promotions by different subsidiaries and divisions of BDD. Where applicable, winners will have their choice of any prize offered at level won. Employees of BDD, its divisions, subsidiaries, advertising agencies, independent judging organization, and their immediate family members are not eligible.

Canadian residents, in order to win, must first correctly answer a time limited arithmetical skill testing question. Void in Puerto Rico, Quebec and wherever prohibited or restricted by law. Subject to all federal, state, local and provincial laws and regulations. For a list of major prize winners (available after 1/29/95): send a self-addressed, stamped envelope entirely separate from your entry to: Sweepstakes Winners, P.O. Box 517, Gibbstown, NJ 08027. Requests must be received by 12/30/94. DO NOT SEND ANY OTHER CORRESPONDENCE TO THIS P.O. BOX.

Don't miss these fabulous Bantam women's fiction titles

now on sale